The Old Book

E J Williams

Bradley Johnson stands outside an antique book shop in Cambridge, England. Weighed down by life's expectation, he trudges through each day, detached from his father and siblings: drifting further from his wife and the person he once was.

Gordon Andrews was the former head of English at Cambridge, and now the proud owner of an Antique bookshop. He shares his residence with his Canadian granddaughter, Alex; a vibrant young woman, and a student at Magdalene College.

The elderly bookstore owner has done his best to move on from a life dotted with sadness, but by chance he meets Bradley, and their families intertwine across two countries to raise secrets from the past.

Success as a Sydney-based lawyer has given Gabi Johnson everything she needs, except the courage to face her father as her true self. Outwardly confident, she is the person that holds the Johnsons together by the barest thread, her strength drawn from her mother Emily, the woman she always wanted to be.

The death of their father brings the siblings together in Australia for the funeral, but the passing of Robert senior is only the vehicle that moves the middles-aged Johnsons towards reconciling their pasts and confronting what they have become.

www.ejwilliamsauthor.com

1

Cambridge, England

Bradley Johnson stood in the bitter cold and peered through the shop window that had been made opaque with dust. The middle-aged man moved his face closer to the glass and squinted. He hoped to catch a sign that would suggest the shop was in fact open, but the dust and the warp that showed the age in which the rectangular panes were created, made it impossible. He hadn't thought to simply push on the door that was only two metres to his left.

Bradley looked down at his damaged book. He rubbed the worn hardcover and then winced at a memory that was filled with bitterness and pain. He had put each page back in order after the scuffle, and as neatly as he could, but they protruded and stuck out from each other in a way that made it rough and most unlike the beautiful book it was, or had been. He pushed the memory away and into the damp and cold Cambridge air that surrounded him. He sighed and then looked to the left towards the door; a sign directly above it read *Andrews Antique Books*.

A bell chattered to signal his entry and also to confirm the shops authenticity. The shop's owner wanted the customers, or patrons as Mr Andrews would say, to feel that they had entered a place of worship—a temple. Bradley felt like he had entered such a place. He paused as soon as he crossed the threshold and caught a scent that he hadn't experienced since he was at school. It made him feel nervous, and he put his hand to his throat to check a tie that wasn't there.

With a quietness that one would display in church, Bradley slowly bent at the knee to place his leather brief case beside an antique hat-stand. He straightened and then held his book a little tighter.

'Good morning.' An aged but firm voice found its way to Bradley through the pillars of literature that stood in uneven columns, like the ruins of an ancient civilisation. The countless volumes were nestled in a valley guarded by mountain-like mahogany shelves, which seemed to domineer a valley full of intrigue.

Bradley searched for the voice. He looked past some books that had been placed on a table with the intent of being shelved, and saw a cardigan covered arm bent at the elbow. He moved his head to change his line of sight and then gave a soft smile. An elderly man, maybe eighty or so, sat on a stool. He held a book in his right hand so the spine faced him, and a pencil in his left. A clipboard rested partly on his lap and partly on the table in front of him, and his eyes darted back and forth, from left to right, like he hadn't quite decided on a paint colour.

'Oh, there you are…hello,' said Bradley. 'I wasn't sure if you were open.'

'Yes, open all day, well most of it. How can I help?'

Bradley looked down at his own hand. 'Do you do repairs?'

'We do...but it depends of course,' replied the elderly man. 'What have you got there?' The man waved his hand slowly towards the book in a fashion that was in place with the surroundings.

Bradley moved forward. He glanced at the high shelves and the even higher ceiling as he stepped carefully. A timber ladder caught his eye. It reached to the highest shelf, and appeared to be on a track. Bradley looked back at the elderly man. *Surely not.*

He reached the spot at which the old man worked and held out the bundle. Bradley felt embarrassed at the state of the book, and being restricted to any purposeful movement, he ran his free hand through his hair. 'Sorry, it's a real mess,' he said.

'Gordon Andrews,' said the elderly man with a slightly closed, but still outstretched hand. He peered over the top of his glasses at the book. His eyes narrowed, and his mind wandered for a moment. He heard sounds, saw images, and was engulfed by fragrances from a time long ago. Lost to another world, Mr Andrews suddenly refocused at the sound of his visitor's voice.

'Bradley Johnson, pleased to meet you Mr Andrews.' Bradley shook Mr Andrews' hand gently, and then passed one of his most cherished possessions over to him.

Gordon Andrews received the tattered book like he had been entrusted with a newborn baby, not with nervousness or fear, but a confident caress that showed years of experience guided by love. He paused and then looked at the book like he would look at an old friend.

'You know I've never been in here before,' said Bradley, still nervous. 'Walked past a thousand times, but never came in.'

Mr Andrews raised an eyebrow and smirked to acknowledge Bradley's statement, but his focus was on the faded blue cover. '*The Pageant of English Poetry*,' he whispered with reverence. He delicately opened the hardcover.

'I put each page in order…I hoped it could be restored…it is very special to me.' Bradley looked at the ground, as an image of his mother Emma filled his mind.

'Indeed,' said Mr Andrews softly. He had heard Bradley, and the words he spoke had struck a chord, but he was somewhere else. Three pages in Mr Andrews saw the faded inscription as he remembered it, "*To my dear Robbie from your loving Mother.*" Mr Andrews' eyes became wet. Below that message was a similar hand, only more visible; it was younger, but not youthful, although it made Gordon feel that way. He closed the book gently and stroked the cloth cover once again.

Bradley stood quietly and watched the elderly man study the book he treasured. He could see Mr Andrews had become emotional. He thought to himself how wonderful it was that someone could be so passionate about what they did that it summoned such emotion in front of a complete stranger. Then, in a moment of guilt, he imagined that Mr Andrews had not felt the emotion he had attributed to him, but was in fact saddened that someone could treat a book in such a way. Bradley felt nervous again and began to shift his feet. Mr Andrews was awoken by the scrape of leather on the worn timber floor and looked up. 'Three weeks…maybe a little longer.'

'Excellent,' stated Bradley. 'Thank you.' He spoke quickly, mostly out of relief, as well as nervousness; he fumbled for his wallet in a clumsy attempt to show his appreciation. 'How much do I owe you?'

Mr Andrews raised his palm to his agitated customer and smiled, he liked Bradley. He imagined he always had; it just struck him at this moment that he had never actually met him, only heard loving stories, and seen him on occasion from the window of his office at the university. The young Bradley would come with his father and brother and sister, twice a week for a family picnic. They would sit on a blanket and clap excitedly as Emma Johnson strode with outstretched arms across the lawn.

'In due course,' stated the university's former head of English, in a soft and friendly voice. He was afraid that a sudden disturbance would shatter the image he held in his mind. In his imagination, Emma looked past a leafless oak and toward him; she smiled, waved, and then the picture faded.

Sobered by the smell of old books, Gordon stood gingerly with a task in mind. He still walked most places but his joints now took a while to cooperate after long periods of sitting. Behind Mr Andrews was a desk. Bradley didn't notice it at first because it was behind a wall of books. Mr Andrews reached over the crest and picked up a business card. He handed it to Bradley. The card was simple, but neat; it displayed a touch of class, much like its owner.

'Thank you, I really appreciate this Mr Andrews…do you mind if I have a look around?'

'By all means Bradley. Let me know if you need assistance.' Mr Andrews pivoted left and then right. He embraced his little shop with a sweep of his arm. 'It's chaos, but it is organised…believe it or not.'

Bradley moved slowly, and casually looked at titles as Mr Andrews took his seat again. The elderly man motioned to pick up the disturbed bundle of poetry that he had last seen years ago, but decided to pick up his clipboard instead when the hope of being emotionless left him. Bradley moved his head in an almost constant rhythm to meet the organised chaos of Mr Andrews reference system, and missed—for the second time—the bookshop owner's connection with his family heirloom.

'You have some wonderful titles here Mr Andrews.'

'Thank you, Bradley.' Gordon shifted in his seat and turned his attention to the middle-aged man perusing his shelves. He let his clipboard rest on the book-covered table in front of him. 'Most of them were here when I bought the business, but I have been lucky to have acquired some real treasures in recent times…from markets would you believe…and through the generosity of some old university friends.'

'You were at the university?' Enquired Bradley, as he ran his thumb across the jacket of a childhood favourite; his mother used to do that before she read to him. It added to the anticipation of the story to come. The cover, in Bradley's childhood eyes would seem to sparkle at his mother's touch; she only picked tales of excitement. For a moment Bradley hoped that the hard cover copy of *Treasure Island* would breathe under his own hand as it had for his mother.

'Yes…though it seems so long ago now.'

'Really!' Exclaimed Bradley. He glanced at the copy of *Treasure Island* in his hand as he acknowledged the coincidence.

'Yes…really,' replied Mr Andrews. He chuckled. 'I haven't always been this old.'

'Sorry, I didn't mean to sound rude...I will take this one please.' Bradley moved towards Mr Andrews with his arm outstretched; the book held as an athlete would hold a baton, eager to pass it on.'

'Ah...a classic,' stated Mr Andrews, as he leaned forward to see the title. 'Five pounds.'

'Five pounds, are you sure?'

'It is my first-time buyer incentive scheme,' replied Mr Andrews. He offered a warm smile and Bradley relaxed.

'Five it is.' Bradley returned the smile and began to search his trouser pocket for his wallet with his free hand. The wallet caught itself on the corner of the pocket; the delay prompted Bradley to say something. 'It was one of my favourites growing up...my mother...well she loved to read to us.'

Mr Andrews didn't reply. He lifted his chin slightly as he was captured by an image of Emma, but he didn't speak. He wanted to say that he had heard stories of the Johnson's bedtime rituals, but he didn't, because he felt he shouldn't. Not yet anyway.

Bradley released a sigh as his trouser pocket released his wallet. 'Sorry Mr Andrews, you must think I am reluctant to part with my money.' Mr Andrews gave another of his warm smiles which had the desired effect. Bradley placed his book on top of another and used both hands to flick past a wad of receipts. *Two tens?* He lowered his face towards his wallet to intensify the search. 'I only have tens sorry.'

'I will find some change.' Mr Andrews turned in his chair towards the partially camouflaged desk behind him.

'No, no keep it.'

'Nonsense.'

'Or mark it down as credit.'

Mr Andrews turned back towards Bradley and took a moment to look at him; taking in more than his visitor could imagine. 'As you wish Bradley…I will expect you back soon to unearth another classic.'

'Yes…I will.' Bradley picked up his copy of *Treasure Island*. 'I would like that.' He glanced around the shop and then tipped the book towards the elderly man. It was a salute of sorts, but also a recognition to himself of the warmth he felt in his presence.

After the bell had ceased its chatter and Bradley had passed from view, Gordon Andrews stood slowly. He shuffled around his books and came to a stop at the desk. He opened a small draw at the back of the antique piece of furniture and removed a letter, stained with age. Gordon lifted one edge of the delicate paper and saw the salutation: *Dear Emma*. Those two words, along with the others, had eventually caused so much pain, but had needed to be written to alleviate the torment that he had felt. As Gordon gently allowed the letter to return to its folded state, he asked himself why he hadn't destroyed what had been his innermost thoughts. Why had he allowed into the open what should have remained in his heart. He answered himself as he always had, with resignation, or an acknowledgment that some things have a life of their own: they act without regard for what may come.

As Gordon Andrews placed the letter into its tomb, he glanced at the corner of a black and white photo that protruded from beneath a forgotten receipt. Gordon closed his eyes, there was no need to draw back the curtain that was the scrap of paper. His jaw clenched as he envisaged his son Thomas. His face set like granite, the young man stared with the confidence of a conqueror, while his eyes glistened enough to reveal a sense of mischief.

Gordon closed the draw; his stomach tightened. Amongst his shop that had become his temple, a place where he had rebuilt his life, lay reminders—side-by-side—of his penance.

2

The rumble of raised voices caused Bradley to stop at the steps that led to the front door of his two-bedroom home in Haymarket Road. *Another battle in the continuous war between mother and daughter*, he thought to himself. He sighed and felt the niceties of Mr Andrew's bookstore leave him for the unease of conflict.

Bradley raised his head and stared at the timber front door with the large, and out of proportion, brass knocker. He contemplated an escape to the *Rose and Thistle* for a pint, but knew that wasn't possible; if he had mentioned it over breakfast that morning, it could have been, but he hadn't, so Karen would have made plans accordingly. As if to confirm his predicament, the smell of pork sausages fried in their own fat wafted from the kitchen; he knew he was committed.

A lover of history, Bradley had previously considered himself to be neutral during these conflicts, like Switzerland, but he had corrected himself; he would eventually get drawn into the battle, to take one side or the other. With more effort than he had started with, Bradley continued his ascent. When he reached the door, he took a deep breath before he turned the handle to enter.

'You are not going to France with Toby and that's final,' yelled Karen.

Bradley flinched.

'Ohh...' Melissa groaned. She felt trapped and frustrated under the umbrella of her mother's constraints. At sixteen she felt that the decision to travel with her boyfriend should be hers, and hers alone. The sound of the front door being opened drew her gaze; the sight of her father's familiar coat gave her confidence to continue. She turned to her mother who had moved to open the fridge. 'Why are you being so difficult...Dad wouldn't be like this?'

Karen spun away from the fridge like she had sensed an intruder. 'It's not up to your...'

'Hello everyone,' interjected Bradley. He wanted to prevent his wife from saying something that she wouldn't regret, but would make him feel uncomfortable. He had learnt to cut his wife off before she confirmed what he already knew; she didn't love him anymore.

'Dinner smells good,' he added as he walked through the lounge room to stand at the arched entry to the kitchen.

Karen didn't acknowledge the complement. She glared at her daughter and then turned back to the fridge.

'Hi Dad.'

'Hi Mel, everything okay?'

Melissa attempted to speak, but was cut off by her mum.

'Where have you been?'

Bradley tensed the muscles in his jaw. He tried in vain to recall the times when coming home from work was pleasant. 'Hello Karen. I went to the bookstore on Bene't Street… remember?'

Karen huffed, she didn't want to say if she did or she didn't, only that she was annoyed.

Bradley moved back into the lounge room and placed his briefcase on the three-seater. He opened it and removed the copy of *Treasure Island*. 'Mel, got a minute?'

Melissa poked her head through the arch and looked at her father before she committed. She was uncertain if her parents had already been in discussion in regards to her proposed adventure through France. *Karen could have rung him at work*, she thought. Melissa often fought with, but never underestimated her mother. Bradley smiled warmly at her and she relaxed.

'Sure.'

Melissa walked cautiously into the lounge room with a disconnected lethargy that teenagers seem to instinctively master. 'What's up?'

'Nothing,' replied Bradley. Over the years he had learned how to disarm his daughter, or allay her anxiety. Maybe that was fairer, because Melissa wasn't overly aggressive, just abrupt; it was in her genes. It developed further after being confronted with endless questions, demands and accusations from her perpetually annoyed mother. Bradley realised that he was under, and had been for a quite a while, the same scrutiny as his daughter.

As he removed the copy of *Treasure Island* from his briefcase, he wondered why he couldn't use the same tactics with his wife as he just had now with his daughter; the two were alike in many ways. 'I got this for you Mel.'

Melissa smiled and Bradley suddenly felt as good as he had in Mr Andrews' shop.

He handed his daughter the well-used hardcover and watched as she allowed her hand to glide over its face. For a split-second Bradley saw his own mother and a tear threatened to form in his eye. If he had one thing in common with Melissa it was their love of books; something, that Bradley had shared with his mum.

'*Treasure Island*, thank you.' Melissa stepped forward and hugged her father like she had when she was younger. 'Thanks, Dad, I will start it tonight.'

'You could probably recite most of it.'

'Probably,' replied Melissa, with an innocence that suggested that she had momentarily forgotten that she was a self-sufficient teenager. Bradley's apprehensions as he had entered the front door had been expelled, and he removed his coat like he was about to take a seat at the *Rose & Thistle*. In a moment of fantasy, he pictured his wife moving into the room to enquire if he would care for a cold beer.

'Dad…Dad!

'Huh,' replied Bradley.

'Are you okay?' asked Melissa. 'You had a strange look on your face.'

'Oh,' Bradley blushed. 'I was…something funny happened at work today, nothing important.'

'So, something actually happened at work,' interjected Karen. She had watched the pleasant exchange between her husband and her daughter and felt spite and jealousy where others may have felt love and pride.

Melissa rolled her eyes, and Bradley swallowed. He knew what his job entailed; he dragged himself to it five days a week. He knew that he had climbed as far as he could and he knew that almost anyone could assess and process, approve or decline, building applications, especially someone who had once studied law at Cambridge. Bradley turned towards his daughter and gave her an uneasy smile. He glanced past her and stared at his wife. She had turned away from them and had begun to pack the dishwasher with an efficiency that screamed resentment.

Bradley could hear her frustrations through the silence, and he understood why. He just thought that they had made the decision to play it safe together, for the sake of their finances, and the baby that they would call Melissa. He couldn't remember the part where it had all been on him, even though his wife's actions for the past six or eight years declared it was.

'Where did you get it Dad?'

Bradley broke away from his wife. 'Sorry Mel...' he pinched the bridge of his nose in between thumb and forefinger. 'That old book shop across from St Bene't's Church.'

'I know that shop, it looks haunted.' Melissa suddenly forgot her mother's rudeness and relaxed. 'If you walk past it and look at yourself in the glass your face contorts.'

Bradley smiled. 'That's because the glass is so old...well not because it is old, but because it was made with distortions in it. It was drawn up in a sort of curtain, slightly thicker in places.

Melissa stared at her dad, she wondered how someone would know such a piece of trivial information, but felt comforted that he did. He seemed to pluck them from thin air. 'You just made that up.'

'I did not...it's true.'

Karen Johnson heard the exchange. A voice from deep inside her wanted to say, *he didn't make it up, he has an encyclopedia inside his head*. A flash of colour danced through her mind and then soared into the air. It looked down on a couple sprawled on a blanket on Jesus Green, beside the

River Cam. The young woman with dark wavy hair smiled at a young man whose eyes sparkled with excitement and possibility. The woman was captivated by him and he was seduced by her. The image faded as did Karen's inner voice. She closed her eyes to push out the hurt and then shut the dishwasher door with a force that made Bradley look past his daughter again.

'Would you set the table Mel? I will give your mum a hand.'

Melissa gave the obligatory roll of the eyes, but caught herself and leaned over to give her dad a kiss on the cheek. 'Thank you for the book, I love it.'

'It was my pleasure.'

Bradley stood with purpose and then clapped his hands in front of his torso. He rubbed them together as if he was trying to manufacture some joy by friction, or conjure a genie who could assist him. 'Can I help Kaz?' Bradley placed his hand on his wife shoulder and glanced at the pot of potatoes on a low boil; she dipped her shoulder slightly; it was enough to move Bradley's hand.

'I've got it,' she said.

'How was your day?'

Karen shrugged. 'Okay.' The question annoyed her. *Cleaned the bathroom, did laundry, and packed shelves at Tesco.* 'Did you pay the gas bill?'

'Yes. That bookshop I went to was interesting. I can't believe that was the first time I have been in there.'

'Sounds nice, did he fix your book?' An unwanted image of Bradley being overpowered and dominated by his brother entered Karen's mind.

'Three weeks.'

'Three weeks! How much will that cost?'

'Not much…Mr Andrews was very nice.'

'We shouldn't be paying for it, Robert should be.'

Bradley shrugged, he felt that he should be the one to pay.

'How many sausages would you like?'

'Oh, whatever you think.'

Karen shot a look towards Bradley that said, *that's not a fucking answer*, and moved to the cupboard to pull out some plates.

'Two,' said Bradley. 'Listen Kaz, that stuff with Mel…I'll have a chat with her. I don't want to see you two fighting…'

'No need, I have already told her no.'

Bradley went to speak but exhaled instead. He left the kitchen, sat at the table and watched Melissa remove place mats from an old-fashioned bureau.

3

Sydney, Australia

Gabi opened the door to her father's unit slowly; it creaked, so she stopped for a second, listened for a complaint, and then continued her entry. A current of cool but stale air washed over her.

She flicked on the lounge room light and glanced at the tidy room, before placing the bag she carried on the coffee table. She walked towards the air-conditioning unit, and then silently cursed the housekeeper for setting it so low. Gabi quickly opened the curtains without looking at the blue waters of Sydney Harbour dazzling under the early morning sun; she did stop to breathe in the salty air after she had opened the sliding door to the balcony of the Kirribilli unit; it never failed to take some tension away.

Much better for your lungs Dad, she said to herself.

Gabi knocked lightly on Dr Robert Johnson's bedroom door, waited a moment, and then entered. Her father sat propped up in bed. There was an oxygen tank on a trolley that sat to the right of a bedside table, which had a framed photo of a beautiful young woman on it; the oxygen mask lay draped over a bracket fixed to the headboard. Her father gazed out the large window, his mind concentrated on a beautiful view, but not the one Gabi could see.

'You're here.' Dr Johnson's voice crackled, and Emma Johnson and the Tumut River vanished from his mind. He coughed, and Gabi moved towards the bed. Her father waved his hand in protest before she had taken two steps.

'It's 6am, and the mask is there for a reason,' said Gabi.

Her father ignored the obvious statement. 'Did you bring my newspaper?'

It was Gabi's turn to remain silent, she brought it every day. She left, and then re-entered the bedroom.

'Here you are Father.'

For the first time that morning Dr Johnson looked at his oldest child and gave the most imperceptible of smiles. He loved her dearly, but he had become irritable and more set in his ways as age and illness took hold; more despondent as each day without his wife had grown beyond a number worth counting. Emma visited his thoughts many times during monotonous days and seemingly endless nights.

'Thank you, Gabi...would some tea be out of the question?'

'Already on.'

He reached out and touched his daughter's arm, as she adjusted his pillows. Her muscles tensed; it wasn't easy for her to see her father like this. He was supposed to be in permanent care, but it is hard to tell a doctor what steps he should take to ward off death, especially when he had the financial means to have a private nurse and a live-in housekeeper. Gabi kissed him on the forehead.

'A piece of toast?' Asked Gabi.

'Just a biscuit,' replied her father, as he opened his broadsheet.

'Nutritious.'

Dr Johnson raised his eyebrows. 'Make it two…I see Johnny has been out walking again, half his luck,' he said as he looked at a photo of Australia's new Prime Minister, striding out purposefully along the harbour foreshore.

'I saw Mr Howard yesterday,' replied Gabi. She placed a breakfast tray over his lap, making sure the support stands were locked in.

'Did he have his tracksuit on?'

Gabi laughed. 'No, he was in the city, surrounded by men in dark suits and even darker sunglasses.' She glanced at her father as she moved back from the tray. She visited her father every morning that she was in Sydney, but his aged and pale face struck her like she had just visited for the first time in months. She suddenly had a vision of a young man neatly dressed. He smiled warmly and spread his arms wide, kneeling to meet the embrace of his little girl.

The middle-aged woman turned suddenly from the bed and covered her tightened lips with a clenched index finger. Her father saw it, but pretended not to notice. He sipped his tea, and then looked out the window towards the harbour. He knew his days were drawing to a close and in many ways, he welcomed it. He hated what life had become after it had given—promised—so much.

The loss of his wife to cancer was a blow he had never recovered from. His family went from a model of love and happiness, striving to achieve, to disconnected and then dislocated. It is mostly thought that teenage boys need a man about the house to grow into strong individuals, but the absence of a caring and loving mother, who was also the arbitrator and communicator, left a gaping hole in their sons' lives.

Dr Robert Johnson's relationship with his sons Rob and Bradley suffered. It was probably the reason why he left Cambridge to start a medical centre in Sydney after Emma had died. He couldn't look at a college, the river, or a student on a bicycle racing along cobblestoned lanes, without thinking of his late wife.

Robert senior had sometimes suggested to himself that he had been too hard on his children, but those thoughts would only conjure comparisons of what his wife Emma went through as a child. She had grown up without both parents, and what he saw as his sons' lack of drive or willingness to persevere, made him abrasive and sometimes dismissive of the two youngest Johnsons. Gabrielle was different: like her mother, she was a fighter.

Gabi cleared her throat. 'When you finish your tea, I will help you change for the day. Maybe you could sit on the balcony.' She began to feel agitated in the confined space of her father's bedroom. She brushed her hand briskly over the quilt, as if she had just made the bed and wanted to make it perfect. 'Do you need to use the bathroom?' Gabi wished she hadn't asked; her father preferred the nurse to do that.

'I am fine Gabi.' He tried to change the subject. 'What time do you start?'

She straightened her skirt to compose herself. '8.30...meeting, but I need to get in before that.'

'Of course,' Dr Johnson coughed; he raised his hand to ward off his daughter before he had even finished.

'Make sure Angela and Lea keep the air-conditioner at a good level, you will get pneumonia dad.'

'I will berate the first one who enters.' Dr Johnson smiled and gestured for her to say her goodbyes.

'Do you want me to get the doctor to call by?'

'I'm already here.' Robert Johnson gave a bigger smile, but it was interrupted by another—longer—bout of coughing.

Gabi heard the front door open and close, the sound of things being placed on the kitchen bench, and then a female voice.

Robert Johnson knew who it was and raised his hands in protest, as high as his condition would allow.

'Sorry I am late Mr Johnson...' Angela entered the room: she stopped abruptly when she saw Gabi, she was intimidated by her. 'Hello Miss Johnson.' The nurse looked at the ground.

'Hello Angela,' replied Gabi. *I hate it when she calls me miss, we're almost the same age.*

Gabi walked towards the bed and kissed her father on the cheek. 'I love you dad.' Dr Johnson nodded. Gabi stood, and went to speak, but stopped herself. She decided it could wait. Her father seemed content, despite his obvious frailty. His mood always changed when they spoke about her brothers.

Feeling a sudden and unexplained urge to stay, she stole a glance at the harbour. 'I can cancel the meeting...and spend the morning here.'

'Go, I'm fine...prosecute someone.' There was a moments silence as Robert looked at his daughter. 'Gabrielle.'

'Yes.' She liked it when her father used her full name. When she was young it meant she was in trouble: now it just made her feel—loved.

'Have I ever told you how much you remind me of your mother.'

Gabi didn't answer, she was wrestling with the wave of emotion that had suddenly engulfed her. The comment from her father meant so much. She had spent her whole life trying to emulate the woman she had admired so much as a child, and then as a young lady. Strong and determined in her professional life, as her mother had been, Gabi felt that she had never quite lived up to the other area in which her mother excelled—family. She had always questioned the personal choices she had made, maybe that's why she kept it secret. That choice made her feel weak in some ways.

'Well, you do,' continued Robert. 'You're a good daughter.'

'Thanks Dad, I wanted…'

'Excuse me Miss Johnson,' interrupted Angela, 'time to take your temperature Mr Johnson.'

Dr Johnson waved at his daughter.

'I will pop in tonight, Dad.' Gabi turned and left, as the nurse's sky-blue uniform eclipsed her view of her father.

4

Cambridge, England

One sip of her latte had washed the tension from Karen's body. The morning had been the same as most; a tedious breakfast, followed by a mad rush to get Mel out the door for school, and then three hours of mind-numbing shelve packing at Tesco. Now, she sat alone at a table for two in her favourite coffee shop, and stared towards the street, relaxed and disconnected from home. She was aware of the two elderly men that were engrossed in a game of chess two tables away, and she had noticed a twenty-something woman—girl really—on a small sofa in the corner. The girl, held the book she read in one hand and at a distance that suggested she was important; the world was hers to take, and her life of study and wearing lopsided berets was just a stone that needed to be stepped before greatness.

Karen had felt like that once, but not anymore. The thought crossed her mind to warn the girl. She thought that a friendly, but honest revelation of what life is really like could help her. She rubbed the side of the glass and decided against it. The girl should find out for herself—she had. The warmth of the coffee transferred through the tumbler and into her own hand; it tried to slide up her arm and replace the coldness. Her mind drifted away from the girl full of Promise and back towards the street.

Coffee shops were Karen's retreat from her life, they allowed her to think in a way that was uncluttered by the vision of dirty plates or crumpled-up clothes. This one, on Mill Road, was her favourite. It was quiet, but not dead; a mix of youthful trends and chess playing resignation. It was the place she came to when she wanted to be alone and as close as she could be to herself. The place on Gwydir Street, with its dull lamps and sophisticated music, was the place she went with her friends. At that place, they usually had some sort of spice in their coffee. They—Karen and her friends—would attempt to reignite the enthusiasm of their past; some found it easier than others, which led to the growing infrequency of their catch-ups.

Two tables away, one of the elderly men chuckled, while the other rubbed his chin to help the process of decision. Karen took another sip of her latte. She watched people slide past the window on their way to something or someone; Karen would often try to imagine where or who. *Was it trivial or important?* She would ask herself. She would often come to the conclusion that it was at least more important than where she was headed. That thought made Karen close her eyes, and she reminded herself to think positively. She had read somewhere that it was important to think positively.

Karen glanced towards the young girl and the shelves filled with books that rested above her. The books made her think of Bradley and she felt a pang of emotion that was hard to define. She hated the tension that had made a home for itself in their house. It hadn't always been like that, but Karen had realised that it had become harder to remember when that was. She looked towards the street again. A mother stopped and knelt in front of her child. She removed a tissue from her handbag and wiped a snotty nose; the child cried, and then they moved on.

Slowly, Karen stood and walked towards the book shelf. She didn't read as much as she used to, just the occasional thriller. Bradley read all the time: in the lounge room, on holidays, in bed; they hadn't had sex in six months, maybe longer.

Karen scanned the shelves. They were a motley collection of hardcovers, with the occasional thin paperback which had probably won its place through its quality. She removed one of those thin paperbacks, Chinua Achebe's *Things Fall Apart*. She studied its cover; she had read it at university when she was young, and like the girl who was suddenly close to her. 'Excuse me,' said Karen out of politeness and unease.

The girl looked up from her book and stared at Karen for a second. Her eyes were brown like almonds and as full of conviction as eyes could be. Karen realised that she wasn't a girl at all, but she wasn't a woman either, not in the tested or tried way in which Karen saw a woman to be—like she saw herself.

She placed her book on her lap. She smiled and Karen instantly felt happy. 'No problem.'

The accent was American, maybe Canadian, Karen found it hard to tell.

'Achebe, thought provoking,' stated the young lady. That's how Karen had decided to label her for now, she was young and seemed pleasant. 'Have you read it?'

'Yes, a long time ago,' replied Karen.

'I did an essay on it last year.' The young lady placed a strand of black hair behind her ear that had escaped from the confines of her beret. Karen looked at her skin, flawless and toned, olive if it wasn't in England—beautiful. 'I'm Alex,' she held out her hand.

'Oh…sorry, Karen. Nice to meet you.' Karen felt awkward, almost shy for a moment, which made her feel ridiculous. 'You're at the university?'

'Yes…English.' Alex held up the book that had been resting in her lap.

A flood of memories chased by regret came to Karen. She remembered her days at Cambridge and how she had dreamed of great things—before she had quit. She turned her face towards the books to ward off the emotion that threatened to well in her eyes. For so long she had lived and been adequately happy with the choices she had made. She also knew that the discontent she now felt had been inside her for just as long. Karen could feel Alex's eyes on her. An aged and worn copy of *Wuthering Heights* caught her attention and she removed it from in between two other worn hardcovers; they seemed unwilling to let it go. Karen touched the cover softly. 'I loved this book when I was your age…I read it over and over.'

Karen turned to look at Alex who had remained silent. She had shown maturity in not having responded to Karen's statement. She had allowed it to lay somewhere between the two of them.

'I have seen you in here before,' stated Alex. She held out her hand. Karen obliged and passed the copy of Emily Bronte's classic to her.

'Oh,' replied Karen. She was not only surprised that Alex had noticed her, but embarrassed that she hadn't noticed Alex. 'It is my getaway, I suppose.'

'Mine too,' replied Alex. 'Wuthering Heights. I still have the copy my grandfather gave me.'

'Really! Karen caught the excitement in her own voice, but then allowed it to flow through her. She motioned to a chair that was unoccupied by a table near her.

'Be my guest.'

Karen grabbed the chair and placed it at a respectable distance. Alex moved her eyes towards Karen's original table. She smirked.

'Oh yes.' Karen moved with purpose and picked up her latte, she placed it on the small round table in front of the sofa and huffed as she sat down.

'Sorted,' said Alex. She laughed. 'Sorry Karen, a friend of mine...an English friend, says that, but I just can't make it work.'

Karen laughed, it felt good. 'Well, I wasn't going to say anything.' She had a sip of her latte, which was now on the cooler side of warm. 'You sound a long way from home Alex, I wasn't sure if it was...'

'Think hard Karen, I will be deeply offended if you say the other place.' Alex mimicked a look of disapproval and then relaxed into a smile that made Karen feel like they were friends.

'Canadian.' Replied Karen quietly. She rounded her shoulders slightly and gave a forced smile like she had braced for the impact of a snowball.

'Correct.'

Karen felt relieved, and then silly.

'Vancouver to be precise.'

'I would love to go to Canada...those mountains.'

Alex smiled and then took a sip of her own coffee, a cappuccino. 'And you Karen? I caught a hint of something that suggests you're not a Cantabrigian...oh my god, I sounded like one of my lecturers.'

Karen laughed. 'Birmingham, many years ago, but it's a long and boring story.' Karen laughed again, but this time nervously. 'You mentioned that your grandfather bought you that book.' Karen motioned towards the novel she had removed from the shelf.

'Yes, I brought it with me…from Canada I mean. I am living with him while I study, so it's crossed the Atlantic twice.'

'He's English?' Asked Karen

'Yes, the most English man I know. It was my grandfather who suggested I apply to study at Cambridge…I was all set to go to B.C.'

Karen gave a puzzled look.

'Sorry…University of British Colombia, it is in Vancouver. Smart choice, right?'

Karen stared at Alex. She smiled in a way that she hoped would encourage her to continue her story. Her day, her attitude, had taken a sudden and unexpected turn, and she liked it; she wanted it to continue. The demands of delusional teenagers and the numbness of a comfortable husband felt so far away, as to be disconnected from what she now felt. It crossed her mind that this new sensation was childish, a whim, something like Melissa's planned adventure to France, but she pushed that idea quickly to one side. For some reason, at forty-five, Karen felt invigorated by someone half her age.

'But no,' continued Alex, 'not for my Grandpa. He wrote me a letter and then called me in the middle of the night, I think he forgot about the time difference. My dad was furious.' Alex giggled to suggest that she enjoyed that part. 'He said to me, *"if you have decided to study English Alexandra, you should come to Cambridge. It is the only choice really"*.' Alex took a sip of her coffee and then pulled both of her legs up on the sofa to sit cross-legged. Karen almost laughed at the thought of her trying something similar. 'I told him about B.C., and even Princeton, but he pretended not to hear me. A week later a large envelope arrived with the application forms…and here I am.'

'It sounds like your grandfather loves you very much.'

Alex allowed her eyes to drop. She gave the faintest of smiles towards her own lap, which told Karen that what she had said was understated.

**

Traffic, motorised and pedestrian, moved with purpose along Regent Street. The weekend was close, but not close enough for the nine to fivers; the government and office workers who looked to Friday's close-of-business, like a pious person would anticipate the coming of a religious holiday. Their increased tempo seemed like a vain attempt to wind the clock forward.

Bradley moved calmly. He had no desire to rush to what he knew would go too quickly anyway. Friday was the day Bradley looked forward to the most; it gave him a sense of relief. Relief in the sense that he had conquered another week, endured what had become the 'norm'. This afternoon he would relax at the *Rose & Thistle* with a pint and *The Times*, as he did each Friday, and escape for a while. Inside the cosy pub, he would sit and listen while his eyes skimmed over print. Men, mostly his age would banter; despair over Cambridge United and then prophesise about the chance of the top-weight in the 3.10 at Newmarket tomorrow. There would be none of the young university rabble that you might find at other pubs, or the privileged sweater draped crowd with a knot tied neatly in front; the patrons were workers, tradesman and the like. Bradley was not one of those, but they seemed to bear his presence. He would enter without fuss, nod hello, order a pint and leave the barmaid, Maggie, a small tip. He would sit with his broadsheet and became part of the furniture.

At home, like work, people spoke at Bradley, not too him. Melissa was pleasant, on occasion, but with the arrival of the teens, and a boyfriend, it was now becoming less common. The purchase of the book from Mr Andrews' shop had been inspired and he had enjoyed the connection with his daughter. It had also diverted the tension created by the proposed, but ridiculous, trip to France.

A thought crossed Bradley's mind. He moved to the side of the pavement to find relief from the constant stream of people. A headphone-clad young man in jeans and track top bumped into him. 'Sorry,' shouted Bradley. He was shocked by the collision which had spun him and his assailant towards each other. Bradley gave an apologetic nod to confirm his sincerity, but the young man replied with his index finger pointed to the sky while he walked arrogantly backwards. Bradley lent against the wrought-iron fence that barricaded Emmanuel College from the busy commute and tried to expel the young man's action from his mind; he felt like he attracted contempt.

He placed his briefcase next to the wheel of a bicycle, one of many that used the fence as a bike rack, and then rolled his injured shoulder to help remove the numbness. He stared towards Downing Street. *I could go to the bookshop instead.* He pulled a packet of mints from his pocket and used his thumb to prise It loose from the foil and paper wrap. *But it's Friday...Karen would ask about the pub?* Bradley placed the mint in his mouth, picked up his briefcase and then darted past an elderly lady and across the road. He walked with intent along Downing, and then turned right at Corn Exchange Street.

**

The bell chattered and Bradley suddenly felt stupid. He asked himself why he had returned to the bookshop a day after he had taken his old book to be repaired, which was a day after the last day in which he had been oblivious to the shop's charms.

You don't need an excuse to visit a bookshop Bradley. Inside his head, a quiet but distinct voice berated him. The voice had been more noticeable of late, it didn't like how controlled Bradley had become. He placed his briefcase next to the hatstand and then searched for Mr Andrews like he awaited to be invited in.

'I am afraid your book is not finished yet, Mr Johnson.' Mr Andrews stood, slightly hunched, behind his antique desk. He removed his reading glasses and began to clean them with a cloth that he had removed from his pocket. 'In fact, I haven't begun.' Mr Andrews laughed at his own joke.

'Oh, I didn't...' Bradley's tongue tripped over itself.

'That was in jest my dear fellow...glad to see you again.' Mr Andrews moved away from his desk and began to navigate through his village of publications. 'How may I help you?'

'Just thought I would have a look around again, if that is alright.'

'Perfectly, that is why I am here...and you are in credit, remember.'

Bradley said yes, even though he had forgotten. 'My daughter loved the book I bought.' Mr Andrews' welcome had allowed his muscles to relax. His declaration about *Treasure Island* had followed without the restrictiveness of thought; thoughts that had always seeked approval of late.

Bradley removed his coat and placed it on an empty hook, directly above his briefcase.

'I am pleased, but also sorry, I should have offered to wrap it. I wasn't aware that it was a gift.'

'No, no need to apologise. Melissa…my daughter, was happy. She had a copy when she was younger…somehow it got lost,' Bradley looked at the ceiling, embarrassed to have heard what he had said. 'Anyway, she was truly excited when I showed her.'

Mr Andrews placed a finger to his chin and then in a light-bulb moment, he raised his hand above his head. 'I think I might have something that you will like.' He turned with the restrictiveness of old-age and made for the far wall. At the back of the shop a door slammed. The elderly man stopped and glanced down an aisle: in the direction of the disturbance. For a second or two he craned his neck, before he suddenly relaxed; something familiar had caught his eye. Bradley's eyes followed where the bookshop owner had looked, and then back at Mr Andrews, satisfied that he did not seem alarmed.

'Now, I am confident what I am after is on this shelf, but you will have to be patient Bradley, my mind is not what it used to be.'

'I'm in no rush Mr Andrews,' replied Bradley, which was a lie of sorts because he only ever spent two hours at the *Rose & Thistle*. A thought came to Bradley. *I could drink at the*

Bath House, it's practically next door...that would work well.'
Another thought suggested he was pathetic.

Mr Andrews stood at the base of the wooden ladder that Bradley had noted on his first visit. Deep in thought, the elderly man allowed the index finger of his right hand to trace along his jaw-line. It paused on his chin before it grasped the timber ladder; he began his ascent.

Bradley stood patiently and then was distracted by an accented voice—American, he had thought.

'Grandpa?'

The voice was soft. It seemed to respect the shop as Bradley did.

'Over here Alex.'

The young lady came into view and Bradley made eye contact. He smiled at her and she smiled back; he felt as though the room had been warmed, and he was lost for a moment in the confidence of her youth. She glided past him, uninhibited—he surmised—by commitment or dependants; allowed, as her walk suggested, to do as she pleased.

'Grandpa!' The serenity was shattered by a cry that Bradley was used to at home.

Bradley jumped back a step, but Mr Andrews didn't falter.

'I told you not to climb that ladder, Grandpa.'

'I am perfectly fine, thank you,' replied Mr Andrews. His tone was calm and measured, like he had been asked if he was warm enough, or had enough to eat.

'You will break your neck one day,' huffed Alex. She realised that her protests were in vain, but she felt compelled to air them.

The elderly man reached the shelf in question and paused. He looked right, but only for a moment, for he was more confident in his memory than he had let on to Bradley. He stared intently at the shelf to his left. 'Got it,' declared, Mr Andrews, oblivious to his granddaughter's prophecy. He placed the book he had searched for in his cardigan pocket; it made the woollen garment sag, so he made sure it was secure before he began his descent. 'Well Alexandra,' Mr Andrews spoke slowly, in time with his steps on the ladder, 'I would much rather go peacefully in my sleep, but if you will have me endure a more dramatic ending…then so be it.'

'That's not what I meant, Grandpa.'

Bradley looked awkwardly around the room. He thought for a moment that he had somehow transferred the negativity from his own home to the sanctuary that was the bookshop; somehow, he had disturbed its tranquillity. Mr Andrews' smile told him otherwise.

'Here we go Bradley…another tale of adventure.'

Mr Andrews gave Bradley a hard cover book that had faded from red to pink with patches and small lines of yellowy-brown where the colour had gone altogether. Bradley glanced quickly at the young lady who stood with her head bowed. She scuffed the timber floor with one of her Adidas joggers, the type you didn't run in. 'Gulliver's Travels…you know I've never actually read this, thank you.'

'Perfect,' replied the bookshop owner, 'you can revisit your youth, Bradley.'

Tired from his climb, Mr Andrews sat on a stool a few paces from the base of the ladder. It had a round seat and four legs, held fast by beautifully crafted crossbars. It was nestled amongst two piles of books that were at a height that was suitable for arm rests. 'Bradley may I introduce my safety officer and granddaughter Alexandra Andrews.'

Alex rolled her eyes towards her grandfather, but then allowed herself to be infected with his charm. She turned to smile at the middle-aged man with her hand outstretched, and Bradley felt the peace of the shop had been restored.

'Alex is fine, how do you do?'

'Bradley Johnson.' They shook hands softly.

'Sorry for my outburst, but my grandfather thinks he is a gymnast.'

Gordon Andrews didn't reply; he smiled and raised both hands from his lap instead, in a sign that accepted the accusation without animosity. 'How was your day, Alex?'

'Good, handed in my assignment.'

'Excellent.'

'I met a lady at the coffee shop.'

'Oh, the coffee shop.' Mr Andrews made a sign for inverted commas. 'Who holds the lectures there these days?'

'Extremely funny Grandpa…she was interesting.'

'They are the best type.'

Bradley watched the exchange between the two people. He guessed that they were probably separated in age by close to sixty years, but joined by something that was stronger than their common surname. 'Thank you again Mr Andrews for going to so much trouble… and it was nice to meet you Alexandra…Alex.' Bradley tripped over the shortened version of the young lady's name after he had remembered the approval to use the shortened version.

'It was nice to meet you too.'

'I do apologise for our little side-show Bradley,' stated Mr Andrews, 'I will have that book repaired as quickly as possible.'

'No hurry, good-bye.' Bradley turned and made his way towards the door. He gave another wave after he had put on his coat and then disappeared under the chatter of the door-bell.

'He seemed nice Grandpa…probably thinks I am a brat.'

Gordon gazed at the door. He acknowledged Alex's statement through raised eyebrows; held in suspension, and then released. 'I knew his mother.'

'Oh,' replied Alex. 'Is that why he visits?'

'No, actually.' Gordon stood. He casually looked around his shop; he looked for something, but nothing in particular. 'He doesn't know.'

The young lady went to speak, but stopped herself. She had wanted to ask, '*why*', but had matured enough over the last year not to ask questions that presented themselves in such an obvious manner. Her grandfather noticed her restraint, it was appreciated, and prompted him to give a little more.

'I didn't feel that it was appropriate.'

Alex raised her eye-lids to reveal more of her almond eyes. 'Oh.'

Gordon turned to look at his granddaughter. His eyes glistened and it struck at Alex's heart.

'Are you alright Grandpa?'

'Perfectly, my dear.' Mr Andrews looked towards the door again. 'What do you say to accompanying an old-man at dinner?'

'I'd love to.'

5

Cambridge

Bradley had almost reached the front door of his home before he noticed something unusual; it was the lack of noise, and it made his pause for a moment. It was a pleasant change from the day before, but it still seemed odd. That is not to say that his wife and daughter fought each day, but there was usually some sound to indicate life, even if it was just the television. Today was eerily quiet and Bradley paused before he reached for the door handle. He looked guiltily at his latest purchase; certain Karen would say something negative. He turned the door handle. *Maybe they have gone out?*

Bradley opened the door; he caught the faintest scent of cigarette smoke. He scrunched his nose. *Karen had quit*, he thought.

'Hello!' There was no answer. Bradley placed his briefcase on the ground and had begun to take his coat off. He glanced to the right and noticed that the television was in fact on, but the sound was muted. He tilted his head and made an unusual contortion of his lips to acknowledge the oddness that he felt. In his peripheral, he caught the shape of a person under the arch of the entry to the kitchen, and he jumped in fright. He dropped his book.

'Shit...Karen it's you. I didn't think anyone was home...I called out.'

Karen stood perfectly still with her hands clasped in front of her torso. The scotch she had gulped before Bradley had entered, still clawed at her chest. 'How was work?' Karen swallowed. It was a dumb question, but she didn't know what else to say; she had wrestled with what was the right thing for the past two hours, after the phone call, but she had been left blank.

She had greeted Melissa abruptly when she had arrived home from school, and then asked her to go to her room when she had felt tears well behind her eyes. Melissa had trudged away confused and Karen had regretted her lack of tact.

'Good…sort of. It's Friday.' Bradley gave an awkward laugh and then bent down to pick up his book. He watched Karen fidget with her hands and then he looked towards Melissa's bedroom as he heard the door creak from down the hall. 'Everything alright Kaz?'

Karen was at a loss as to how to start. Years ago, she would have taken her husband by the hand, and did whatever had felt natural: held him, kissed him, there was no need for a script then, but she needed one now. 'Your sister called.'

'Gabi?' Bradley gave a puzzled look, he hadn't heard from Gabi in over two months, and then his instincts screamed at him. His voice went up an octave. 'Just now…did she want me to call her back? Did…'

'I have some bad news.' Karen inhaled deeply and then she looked at the ceiling.

'Kaz?'

'Your father passed away…I am so sorry Brad, so sorry.'

Bradley looked at his wife like she had said something he hadn't quite understood. He moved to the back of the sofa and placed his hand on it for support. Karen felt inadequate and ill-equipped to render the necessary compassion. She took a step towards her husband and then inexplicably stopped. Her inaction tore at her sole more than the news of Mr Johnson's passing.

'Gabi said he passed peacefully…in his sleep.'

'Was he sick…? I mean…' Bradley cut himself off. The question had highlighted his relationship with his father, or the lack of one. He knew he had been unwell; it was the last thing he and his sister had spoken about. Bradley had thought it was just the flu, the type that knock elderly people about more than the young; he hadn't enquired beyond that, the realisation made him feel sick.

He moved to the dining table and sat in one of the upholstered timber chairs. Released from stagnation by Bradley's movement, Karen walked quickly into the kitchen. She poured her husband a scotch and then sat beside him at the dining table. She felt some tension leave her body, this seemed more normal to her. Husband and wife, side by side in a moment of need.

Karen reached out and placed her hand on Bradley's. He looked up at her, lost. 'I really am sorry Brad, I know…well I know this would be hard for you.'

Bradley caught the inference that Karen had stopped herself from making. He took another sip of scotch. He knew that he and his father did not see eye to eye—barely spoke in fact. He knew, and had expected the news to come one day; his father was ninety, but he hadn't expected to feel how he now felt—vulnerable. 'I should ring Robert.'

'Dad?'

Karen looked up first, and then Bradley followed. Karen stood and walked over to her daughter. 'Aunty Gabi rang, your grandfather passed away Mel, I am sorry for being the way I was when you got home.' Karen was surprised at the apology she had given, but pleased that she had allowed herself to give it. She hugged her daughter and the young girl sunk into the embrace. Bradley joined them.

'Are you okay Dad?'

Lost for words, Bradley kissed Melissa on the forehead. He wasn't okay, which was normal for someone who had lost a parent. What had rendered Bradley dumb, and then racked him with guilt, was that he had always told himself that he would be okay without his father.

**

'I should call Robert,' stated Bradley. He spoke to himself as much as he did Karen and Melissa. He turned to Karen and then suddenly drank the remainder of the scotch. He paused for a moment to look at the crystal tumbler, an engagement present from his father; Bradley almost choked on the irony. Karen saw tears form in her husband's eyes. She placed her hand on his knee.

'That would be a good idea…Gabi would have called him by now.'

Bradley clenched his jaw and stood from the chair, he had had no contact with his brother since they had fought and he was nervous about the call. He shook his head at the ridiculousness of his fear. *Your dad just died. You had a scuffle with your brother, so what…, toughen up!* The voice was sharp, just like his fathers, and it bit into him painfully. 'Should I use the landline or mobile?'

Karen shrugged her shoulders; she smiled, but her heart sighed at her husband's indecision and then tightened at her own bitterness. In this moment of sadness, she realised she barely recognised the person in front of her; her husband, who was once dynamic and spontaneous. 'It doesn't matter…try the landline.'

'Okay.'

Bradley lifted the receiver from the telephone that hung on the wall by the entry to the kitchen. He punched three numbers and then paused to recall his brother's number in Hunslet. Karen stood and walked over to the sofa where Melissa sat, as Bradley remembered the remaining numbers.

Karen smiled at her daughter and then kissed her on the top of her head, and then sat beside her. Melissa smiled uneasily; her disposition had become tense since she had instinctively nestled into her mum's embrace. She wondered why she had suddenly felt different, but she couldn't find an answer, so she turned her gaze towards her dad. She wanted to hug her mum, to release the emotion she felt from her dad's sadness, but the wall that she had built in her mind had grown to a height that was not easily scaled. Although it lacked any real foundation, built with bricks cast from trivial and impetuous matter, it was there nonetheless. Karen felt the pain of disconnection and then turned her gaze to Bradley as well.

'Hello Jan, it's Bradley...thank you I appreciate that.'

Karen and Melissa listened to one side of the conversation, as they watched Bradley. He stared at his shoe. He raised the toe and then allowed it to fall. He repeated the action in a rhythm that was slow and deliberate.

'Is Robert there? Oh...really, okay. I didn't realise, no that's quite alright...I thought we might travel together...yes, I will try his mobile. Thank you, Jan, I appreciate that...bye.' Bradley placed the receiver back gently. He turned towards the lounge.

'What happened?' Asked Karen. 'Wasn't he there?' Karen was all too familiar with the tension that had existed between Brad and Robert, she corrected herself, had always existed, but she couldn't imagine him not talking at a moment like this.

Bradley wiped his face with his hand that seemed to attempt to erase his anxiousness. 'He has left already...for Sydney...well he's gone to Manchester first.'

'Did Jan say what flight? He couldn't have left yet...maybe...' Karen stopped herself. She had attempted to be helpful, but she had begun to sound frantic.

'She didn't say. Just said that their neighbour had driven him. She sounded a bit confused...said it all happened very quickly.' Brad gave a chuckle weighted with discomfort. 'You know Rob.'

'When will you leave Dad?' Melissa asked the question that she felt would have got a straight and direct answer. Her dad had lost his dad. She had imagined herself in the same situation, with bags half packed while she yelled at her mum for her passport. She didn't have a passport, but she knew her dad did.

'Not sure Mel...soon.' Bradley looked quizzically at Karen. He seemed to ask if he should go, and could he go at the same time.

'We have our credit card,' stated Karen. She stood from the sofa and walked to their bedroom. The card was for emergencies and she kept it in a money box with some other valuables. It had a lock, but the key was always left in it; there had been a few small emergencies over recent months, a facial and a new handbag, she had dreamed of a *hiatus* in Spain.

As she walked, Karen felt her stomach tighten. She knew Bradley had to go to Australia, his father had died, but the cost of the trip would fall on her like an extended sentence. She felt confined within her day-to-day life and a maxed-out credit card would take away the moments—over coffee—when she thought of escape. She was surprised when an image of Alex leaped into her mind.

Karen walked back into the lounge room and handed the credit card to Bradley without speaking. She turned for the kitchen, having decided she would pour herself another small scotch. She stood at the kitchen bench and took a deep breath. She was overcome with feelings that had nothing to do with her father-in-law's death. The pressure on her chest, and all over her body was intense, it held at bay a being that lay trapped within her. It was not right to be consumed by her own needs at this time, and she felt ashamed, but she could feel it. It moved erratically within her, trapped by her skin that itched, and the life that held her hostage. She took a mouthful of scotch. An involuntary sob escaped as he swallowed; it caused some of the liquid to dribble down her chin. She wiped it off just as Bradley appeared beside her.

'It's okay Kaz.' Bradley placed his arm around his wife and drew her to his chest. A tear slid down his cheek, not so much in recognition that his father had died, but that his wife had mourned him. For Bradley, Karen's act of emotion had raised the question as to why he hadn't cried or hit something. Strangely, it also gave him a sense of strength that he was able to comfort his wife. 'Everyone handles death differently,' he said.

Karen allowed her husband's words to pass through the air without challenge. She couldn't say, *I'm sorry, but I wasn't thinking about your dad*, so she rested her head on Bradley's chest while the despair relented to the slow burn of the alcohol. 'I'm really sorry about your dad.'

'Thank you Kaz…it doesn't seem real.'

With one hand, Karen wiped one eye, and then the other. She gently moved away from Bradley. She glanced over her husband's shoulder and saw Melissa. She sat cross-legged on the sofa and flicked at the pages of a magazine for the relief the action gave her, not for any desire for knowledge or entertainment.

'Sorry about that…I could do with a drink.' Karen picked up her glass, she looked at her husband with raised eyebrows.

'Yes, I'll have one…and don't be sorry. I was so lost in my own thoughts; I didn't think how you might feel.'

Karen's lips moved slightly to form a smile that became a grimace. *Is life that cruel,* she thought. *Are we that disconnected...what happened?*

'I suppose I need to book a flight,' said Bradley.

'I will call a friend of mine...she's the manager at Flight Centre. She might get us a cheap flight.'

**

Double Bay, Sydney

The morning sun highlighted the golden sand of Double Bay's secluded beach against the brilliant blue of Sydney Harbour. Gabi sat on the balcony of her luxury apartment. She had watched a man as he repeatedly threw a ball into the water for his dog to fetch, but now she looked beyond them, over Darling Point and to the sky-scrapers of North Sydney. She allowed her eyes to fall to where Kiribilli would be; she should be there now, delivering her father's newspaper, and making him a cup of tea.

Instead, she sat alone, except for the naked body still asleep in her bed. They had made love last night, if you could call it that; Gabi had felt the need to release something, as opposed to giving. She looked through the large glass window and the white crumpled sheets that lay scattered due to the summer heat; her lover's skin was tanned and toned, a rope of paler skin marking what swimming costume the younger woman chose to wear.

Gabi stared at her, but felt nothing at this point in time. She looked back to the beach, the man and his dog had disappeared. Her thoughts drifted to the cold room and metallic trolley where she had gone to identify her father in the early hours of Wednesday morning. She had gone back to see him on Tuesday night, as promised, but he was sound asleep. She had spoken to the housekeeper, for a while, and then kissed her father on the cheek before leaving.

She looked into the distance and tried to think of the last thing they said to each other. It was all a blur, her phone call with Karen leapt into her mind, and just as quickly she heard her father say: *you're a good daughter*, and she burst into tears.

The tears suddenly turned into a groan of frustration. Gabi tucked her legs to her chest and held them there tightly with her interlocked arms, so that her heels rested on the edge of her chair. She pushed her face against her knees. Images of her parents flashed in and out of her mind.

She felt alone: her life had revolved around work and looking after her father. The fact that she hadn't had the courage to show her true self to those around her, made her question the feelings she had for the woman in her bed. She thought she loved Natalie, but if that was the case her father would have known her name, and asked about her from time to time, regardless of whether he approved.

Gabi was alone, but there would be no more tears. She raised her head and wiped each cheek with broad strokes of her hands. *Bradley and Rob will need support.* Her father's words rung in her ears like he was sitting beside her. She thought back to the first of many times he had said it.

He had telephoned her at the college and said that he had wanted to talk to her at home. It was Friday afternoon, and she had planned to go to London with some friends, but he had insisted, so she had made the fifteen-minute bicycle ride in misty rain to the Johnson's Cambridge home.

Over the salty Sydney breeze, Gabi could smell the mustiness of damp and decaying leaves. She stood at the front door of her parents' house; she could see the rose bushes either side of the wrought iron hand rails Her father had simply said *thank you for coming*, once he had opened the door. His expression had been pained, and Gabi had simply followed him to his office when he had turned and walked away.

The warmth of central-heating had replaced the dampness from outside, but Gabi could still remember the chill that had sat between the leather upholstered chairs, and dark mahogany bookshelves of her father's office.

The words, *your mother has cancer*, had drifted around the room while Gabi had sat without expression. She had remained unmoved for such a time that her father had stood and moved from behind his desk. He had thought he could be more in control there, he had not come to terms with the news himself; Gabi would eventually realise that he never would.

Gabi remembered how her father had sat next to her. There had been a silence while he had mustered his strength. *It is pancreatic cancer,* he had said, and Gabi had looked towards her lap and began to pick at the skin around her fingernails. Her father had tried to relay what the doctors had told him, but he had broken down, and she had finally been shaken from her trance to comfort him. She had never seen him cry after that. She had only witnessed blood-shot eyes and numbed expressions caused from unnatural doses of strain.

She could see the leather-bound books shelved perfectly against the wall of her father's office as she sat on the balcony of her Double Bay apartment. *Bradley and Rob will need support*, he had said, when he had looked at her with an expression of hopelessness.

The details that her father had not been able to relay would find their way to Gabi soon enough. Her mother had died within six months, and Gabi had become a surrogate parent to her brothers, while trying to continue her own life as a law student.

Gabi felt a soft kiss on her cheek, which allowed the sounds of Sydney harbour to flood back in.

'How are you feeling?' Asked Natalie. The thirty-something woman had asked Gabi the same question over the last couple of days. *Fine*, was the only answer she had received.

6

Heathrow, London

A man lay sprawled on the last chair in a row of plastic seats that looked to be deliberately manufactured to be uncomfortable. His mouth gaped and his glasses sat half way down his nose. A young boy, about five years old, stared at him for a moment before his mother dragged him away in fear, not of the man, but of what her son might do. Bradley gave a short, but heartfelt laugh. It felt good, and he realised it was the first time his heart had felt light since the news that his father had passed. He suddenly felt guilt for having allowed himself to forget his grief.

He had cleared customs without too much fuss; the snake-like queue had been the worst part. One man, two places up from Bradley, had been taken aside by the authorities. Bradley had watched the situation unfold until a customs officer had made eye contact with him. From then, he had looked mostly at the ceiling or the far wall, and then his shoes. He had bought a book, and a coffee once given the all-clear, and then sat in the departure lounge to await his flight. Karen's friend had got him a good deal with only one stop, but it had meant waiting two days to depart. Robert had a forty-eight-hour start, but maybe he had taken the first available—whatever the route.

Ten years ago, the last time he had flown to Australia, Bradley had endured a thirty-eight-hour trip, with two stops.

Bradley's attention was taken by three young men who marched into the boarding lounge like everyone would be excited to see them. He hated people like them, and it wasn't because of their loud Australian accents, which both irritated and embarrassed him at the same time. After all his parents had been Australian, and so was he, even though he considered himself British. It was their loutish behaviour that irked him.

A thought struck Bradley that the young men had Actually done their best to imitate apes. He continued to stare at them, and in his mind, he quickly retracted the slight he had imposed on apes. In the documentaries he had watched, male apes seemed to sit with poise and grace. Bradley opened his book and pretended to read, he prayed to God that he wouldn't be seated next to them on the flight.

The thought about the seating arrangements had made Bradley think about something Karen had said to him on the drive down from Cambridge to Heathrow. He had enjoyed the drive; it had been the most time they had spent alone together in a while. It had reminded him of the impromptu trips they used to take when they were young. On one of those trips Karen had almost caused an accident when she had given him head while Bradley navigated the A1. But that was a long time ago. The last time he had suggested Karen do something similar—not in a car—she had laughed and then turned on the television that sat on a collapsible stand at the end of their bed.

Bradley shook the negative thought from his mind. Karen had suggested that it may have been a blessing that he and Robert hadn't been able to travel together. Bradley had taken offence at first, but then conceded that she was right. A plane cramped with people and stale air was not the place to resolve their differences. She had said that being in Australia, with Gabi, and in the reflective environment of their dad's funeral, might be a better place for them to at least talk.

Bradley stared at the blur of black letters and words on the page in front of him. *There is nothing to talk about*, he said to himself. *The book is his, but he doesn't deserve it.* Bradley was racked by the childishness of the whole situation, but fortified by the idea of what the book meant to him—what it60epressented. *It isn't his…really. Left to him it could have ended up anywhere, lost.*

A chime came through the public-address system was followed by a calm and measured female voice. 'British Airways Flight one-five for Singapore and Sydney is ready for boarding at gate five, please have your boarding pass ready.'

Bradley remained seated while the majority of people stood as one, just like a congregation did at church, prompted by a certain word or phrase the priest had uttered. As a child Bradley had never been able to remember the key words that would make him appear as a devout Christian, so was often left slightly, but noticeably behind on the cold pews.

'Could passengers with seats in rows forty-four through to fifty-six please approach the counter with their boarding passes ready.' Unlike a congregation, many people collapsed, without care for how it may look, back into their uncomfortable plastic seats, like hessian sacks full of loose potatoes. The discomfort and stress of air-travel had begun, as always, before take-off.

Bradley closed his book and looked at the cover. He thought of his grandfather who had died long before he was born. On the cover of the book a soldier carried another on his shoulders. The boisterous Australians, in their disappointment at not being called, jostled and tried to annoy each other. Bradley read the title, *Don't Forget Me Cobber (The Battle of Fromelles)*, by Robin S Corfield, it was one of the few books he hadn't read on the subject. The images, one in Bradley's mind of a generation lost to needless sacrifice, and the one in his line of vision were so detached, yet so strangely attached to appear as clueless re-incarnations. Both youthful and in search of adventure; unaware of the world around them, one called to war, the other secure in peace.

**

Karen turned into Mill Road and found a car space in a pay-and-display. She smiled. *That was almost too easy.* The drive to Heathrow had been pleasant enough. They had talked more than usual, which was nice, but Karen had wrestled with the notion on the way home that she had felt a sense of relief when Bradley had stepped out of the car and insisted that she didn't see him off. She had protested out of politeness, but then quickly added that the airport carparks where excessively priced. Bradley had agreed, and then awkwardly poked his head through the half-opened driver side window after he had removed his suit case from the boot. They had kissed, pecked would be a better description, and promised to call, then she had driven off.

Mill Road was busy with mid-morning traffic. The air was cool, but not cold. A hint of moisture was carried on the soft breeze that gently pushed greyish clouds apart. It allowed the sun to glisten on the pavement. It was wet from rain that fell in the time she had been away. The wet roads and pavements gave the surrounds a feel of freshness, just like Karen felt; she felt like she had re-entered a different Cambridge. She knew it was childish, but as she approached the coffee shop, she hoped to find Alex there.

The smell of freshly ground coffee seduced Karen as she entered the cosy café; it enticed her, drew her into a state of mind that she thought had died long ago. She glanced casually around the small room. She smiled at everything and nothing in particular while she looked for Alex. One of the chess players was there; Karen recognised him as the cautious one, the man who deliberated over his moves. He nodded at Karen and smiled with sincerity. She replied with a hesitancy that did little to hide her disappointment at Alex's absence.

'May I help you Ma'am?'

A calm and cool voice broke Karen from her preoccupation with Alex. She turned to face the young man behind the cedar counter; handsome, except for the ring in his nose.

'Sorry…soy latte please.'

'To have here?'

Karen nodded. The thought to leave had invaded her pleasant mood, but she had quickly expelled it. She had been coming to, and enjoying, the coffee shop for a long time before she met Alex. Their introduction had just added a new dimension to the significance of her hideaway.

'£2.65 please.'

Karen gave the young man the correct change and then moved to her regular seat. She listened to the metallic sound of the cash register, as it succumbed to the gravelly, but agreeable sound of coffee beans being crushed into powder. At ease, she placed her handbag on her lap. She smiled at the elderly man again, but with more consideration than before. He smiled as he had, and then spun sharply as the sound of the door being opened caught his, and Karen's, attention. The chess player raised his hands in mock protest while his chess partner shuffled slowly through the door;

Karen, charmed by the boyish exchange, removed her copy of *Wuthering Heights* from her bag that she had packed specifically for the trip.

The texture of the worn hardcover, its contradiction between the smooth and frayed, conjured images of her youth. She felt, and saw, through hopeful eyes a world that had seemed to offer so much.

'Soy Latte Ma'am.'

Karen turned slowly towards the barista; partly awakened from her daydream by the sound of his voice, but still somewhat intoxicated by the feeling of freedom that comes when a married couple are parted for a short time.

'Thank you.'

Karen tore the top off a sugar sachet and then was startled by a sharp and repeated tap on the shopfront window. She looked up to see Alex. The young lady smiled to reveal her perfect white teeth. She stopped her Morse code and turned it into a wave that was just as frantic. Karen could feel her cheeks flush; Alex's enthusiasm was as contagious as it was beautiful. She signalled with an open palm to the empty chair opposite her; Alex nodded, and then moved swiftly through the door.

A gust of air caused the elderly chess players to shuffle in their seat. It was the strongest protest they could think of without being rude.

'Hello!' Alex greeted Karen like a long-lost friend. Karen allowed her warmth to penetrate every part of her body.

'Hello Alex, have a seat.'

Alex let her canvas satchel slip from her shoulder to rest on the floor beside the table. 'Thank you…I'll just grab my caffeine hit.' Alex looked at the barista, who eagerly awaited her order. He, like Karen, had wondered when she would come in.

'The usual Alex?'

'Thanks Ben.'

Alex moved to approach the counter, but was prevented by Karen's raised palm. 'I'll get it,' demanded Karen.

'Thanks Karen, but…'

'I insist Alex…I know what it's like to be a student and strapped for cash.'

'Thank you, that's very kind.'

'Not at all.' Karen stood and walked to the counter. '£2.65?'

Ben, the barista, nodded sharply and then accepted the money for Alex's coffee. He hadn't appreciated Karen's act of generosity in the way it was intended; it had thwarted probably his one opportunity to speak to the most attractive—the nicest—girl he had ever met. Karen turned back to the table oblivious to Ben's torment, as he hit the stainless-steel coffee filter a little harder than usual on the timber bench.

'Thanks Karen, you didn't have to do that.'

'My pleasure.' Karen took a sip of her latte. 'Finished classes for the day?'

'Yes…' Alex rolled her eyes.' The last lecture was sooo, bad. I have this one lecturer…most of them are good.' Karen smirked at Alex's disclaimer. '…But this one.' Alex paused to find the right word.

'It can be that way,' offered Karen as an aid.

Alex turned her head slightly like she had just remembered something. She joined Karen's last statement with something she had said when she first walked in. 'Did you study at university?'

Karen nodded for a yes.

'Really…what…where?'

Karen smiled and pointed to the table. 'Here.'

Alex sat a little straighter in her seat. 'Cambridge?' She looked at Karen bewildered; it could have been taken as doubt, but it was in fact, intrigue.

'Surprised Alex?'

'Yes…no, I mean…'

'It's alright Alex,' Karen jumped in to save her new friend, 'I don't exactly look like the scholarly type. It was a long time ago.'

'What did you study?'

'English…like you.'

'No way…that is so cool. You can tutor me.' Alex looked up; she had caught Ben out of the corner of her eye.

'One regular cappuccino Alex,' stated Ben. He had slipped regular in to lengthen the sentence and therefore his exchange with the young uni student.

'Thank you, Ben.'

'Can I get you anything else?'

'No, I'm fine. Thank you.'

Ben waited a second before he dragged himself away.

'He likes you.'

'Huh?'

'The coffee guy…Ben.'

'Oh…I doubt it.'

'He didn't seem to be bothered if I needed anything else.' Karen raised her eyebrows and Alex cringed internally. She used the coffee shop as a retreat, away from the university. She had a boyfriend, but he was back home in Canada. For the local men that made her as good as single, and she was often asked out, to the point where it had become annoying. Now her sanctuary was under threat and she looked for something to shake-off Karen's assertion.

'Yeah, but you're old enough to be his mum.' Alex leaned forward and deliberately widened her eyes at the middle-aged woman, before she relaxed into her seat and took a sip of her cappuccino.

Karen's surprise at Alex's boldness quickly gave into laughter. 'You cheeky little sod. I may be mature,' Karen sat a little straighter, 'but I can still...' Karen stopped herself. She wasn't sure if she could. 'Maybe I should be pleased he didn't offer me a senior's discount.'

'Still what...?' Alex's question buzzed between the two like a bee. 'I was only kidding,' she added.

'No, you weren't,' replied Karen with a smile that told Alex that she accepted that she was.

'I just wish I could have a conversation with a boy, without them asking me out.'

'Doesn't sound all that bad.'

Alex ignored Karen's rebuttal. 'Or my favourite: 'Wanna hook-up?' Alex took a sip of her coffee. She used it as a buffer between topics; she wanted to get back to Karen's university days. 'So, tell me more about Cambridge back...'

'…In the dark ages?'

'No…I mean it would have been different. No laptops…or cell phones.'

'Yes,' replied Karen. Her voice tapered off, as her mind drifted back to 1982. *Come on Eileen* began to play inside her head, and she could smell the stale tobacco smoke that clouded the pub in which she stood. She saw Bradley. She had never forgotten the first time she saw him, which made their current staleness all the more difficult. His face, on that evening, and for many more, had been exuberant and confident; carefree, as he had slapped his mate on the back. The action had spilt a quarter of his mate's pint.

Alex curiously watched her new friend. She looked deep into greyish-brown eyes that had become glazed over, and wondered what had suddenly trapped Karen into reminiscence. She followed the faint lines of skin, that she knew were called "crowsfeet", and thought of her mum. She hadn't spoken to her, or her father in two weeks. She cleared her throat.

Karen shook her head slightly. 'Sorry…yes it was very different.' Karen took a sip of her latte to compose herself. The song, the tobacco smoke, and Bradley faded from view. 'I was a million miles away. You're right, there were no laptops, our hands ached from writing. I had a callous on my finger for years.'

Alex smiled, but didn't speak.

'And there were definitely no mobile phones…, or cells, as you call them.'

'Sorry,' replied Alex, 'I can't shake that one.'

'The lines for the phones were quite annoying actually…I was at Girton.'

'My friend Sarah is there,' stated Alex with an enthusiasm that seemed to raise her from her seat. She relaxed quickly, as if she had been suddenly reminded by her conscience of the immaturity of innocent youth, something she tried hard to disguise. She wanted to be taken seriously.

Alex looked towards the elderly chess players and smiled. She enjoyed their presence; they were part of the reason she came there so often. They added to the shop's charm and were reminiscent of the travel brochures she used to stare at as a child. They depicted scenes in Italy—not England— on the Almalfi Coast. Cobbled lanes surrounded by ancient buildings, guarded by elderly men who played chess, or scopa, as she had discovered on her holiday last year.

'Does Sarah study English?'

Alex shook her head, and then took a quick sip of her coffee. 'History…that's my minor actually.'

'My husband loves history,' stated Karen with a groan that suggested to Alex that Karen hated it. 'If he is not reading about it, he is watching a documentary on something that happened God knows when.'

Alex sipped her cappuccino, the silence allowed Karen's comment to recede from prominence like a wave that falls back into the ocean. She glanced at the chess players who were still like statues, deep in thought. 'What does your husband do?'

'Works at the council…approves building applications, things like that.' Karen's stomach tightened. The mere mention of Bradley's job made her tense. She realised that it was unfair, the job was secure, and there were many worse, but she felt what she felt.

'That's interesting,' replied Alex politely.

'Pays the bills.'

Karen looked down at her lap. She felt the strained emotion that was bottled up inside her, leap and thrust inside her body, just like it had when Bradley had mistaken her tears for grief. It surged, but was arrested by Karen in her throat. She tasted the bile and swallowed hard; too hard not to be noticed.

Alex was instantly concerned and acted as her youth and nature would dictate. 'Is everything alright Karen?'

Karen didn't answer, she fumbled for her handbag and then searched frantically for a tissue. She found one used and crumbled amongst make-up containers that clattered like pencils in a case. She raised her face towards the ceiling and dabbed her eyes, while Alex placed her hand on her other forearm. Quickly, Alex grabbed Karen's untouched napkin and passed it to her.

'Thank you,' said Karen. She let out a sorrowful laugh. She felt embarrassed by her display of emotion. It was one thing to do so at home, in front of Brad and Melissa, even yell, as she often did, but she preferred to keep her cool in public.

'What's wrong…would you like to talk about it?' Asked Alex with sincerity.

Karen considered it. She almost said, *I feel trapped…like I can't breathe.* She almost blurted that, *she wasn't sure if she loved her husband anymore,* but she didn't, she stopped herself as the words curled her tongue to make it feel like it was cramped.

Alex touched Karen's arm again. Karen closed her eyes. The connection felt…she was lost for words.

Karen opened her eyes again. She felt calm now, but still embarrassed, and then slightly ashamed for what she was about to do. 'I am sorry about that Alex, but my husband's father died…he flew out for Australia this morning. I just got back from Heathrow.'

'I am so sorry Karen, that is so sad.'

Karen shrugged; it was all she could think of.

'Thank you, Alex, that is very kind of you. My father-in-law was quite old, but it is still a shock.'

Alex was surprised that her thoughts drifted to her grandfather and not her father, as she considered loss. At her age it was hard to examine. 'Do you feel like another coffee Karen?'

'I do,' answered Karen without delay. She felt so comfortable around Alex when she just spoke, and didn't think about what would be deemed socially acceptable. She had acknowledged that Alex was young enough to be her daughter. She had even asked herself, in the darkness of her bedroom, if through the enjoyment of Alex's company, she had begun some sort of mid-life crisis, like a man who suddenly bought a red sports car. She knew that she hadn't, and wouldn't even be tempted to have the conversation with Melissa that she had almost had—wanted to—with Alex.

'I will get them this time,' stated Alex. She rose from her seat. Ben, the Barista, looked up from his cleaning duties. His eyes widened with his change in fortune.

'No Alex, I will…'

'I insist,' replied Alex, repeating what Karen had said to her earlier.

Alex sat back down after paying for the coffees. She smiled at Karen but didn't say anything. Karen felt she should…at least to push the negativity of her emotional display out of the café.

'So, I was at Girton...you are?'

'Magdelene,' replied Alex.

Karen smirked. 'You wouldn't have been there in my day...men only.'

'I know, that is so crazy...apparently they protested and did all sorts of ridiculous things. It kind of makes me more determined to do well, which is a bit silly, but I can't help feeling that way. I want to show that women can do as good, and better.'

'Good on you, I think it is a perfect way to show those old fuddie duddies how stupid their rules were,' said Karen.

Alex's face broke into a broad smile that threatened to break into laughter.

'What?' Asked Karen.

Alex leaned back a little to allow Ben to place her coffee on the table. 'Fuddie duddie...where did you get that from?' Alex watched Karen blush. 'I'm going to call grandpa that.'

'Thank you for reminding me of my age again Alex,' replied Karen. She smiled warmly before picking up her own coffee.

7

'We should just fucking go anyway.'

'We can't Mel, my parents said no,' replied the teenage boy wrapped in a black track top; his legs, which were tucked up to his chest, were clad in black jeans, 'and so did yours.'

Melissa moved closer to her boyfriend on the sofa. She put her arm around his shoulders, Toby moved away slightly. It was a reflex action to keep an uninterrupted view of the television. Suddenly he remembered boyfriend-girlfriend etiquette and awkwardly put his arm around her. He kissed her and then stole a glance at the screen. Melissa pretended not to notice, but fell back into the sofa, disappointed with Toby's actions.

'Well we have to do something; I am sick of this shit-hole.'

Toby shrugged and flicked his mop of sandy-brown hair from his eyes. 'Why do you want to go to France anyway? They're all pricks.'

'That's mature, the French have class…and beautiful clothes.'

'They think they are better than everyone else, and they stink. I shouldn't have asked Mum, she will probably start getting sus now and ask more questions…it was your idea anyway.'

'Ohhh,' Melissa stood up in a huff and paced quickly towards the kitchen. Toby moved his head left and right as the blur of Melissa's body eclipsed the television.

Melissa opened the fridge door and took out a can of cola. Angry at her boyfriend, she moved over to the sink and took a clean glass from the rack which held the mornings washed dishes. She looked out the window and stared at the scattered grey clouds. She thought of her father and wondered if he had taken off yet, she knew she would miss him. She looked for a plane amongst the patches of blue, and then felt childish for doing so.

When her parents had said they would be leaving early for Heathrow, Melissa had almost instantly decided that she wouldn't go to school that day. She had calculated that her father would need to be at the airport three hours before the flight. She had heard that everyone saw their wife or husband off, even after they had disappeared behind the partition; people hung around and had a coffee, she assumed, until the plane took off. With a stop for fuel and coffee on the way home, she had reasoned that Karen would be gone all day. That's when she had sent a text message to Toby.

Tired of the view from her kitchen window she focused on the cola can that she held. She stared at the well-known trademark, slowly twisting the object, as if the scrolling letters would reveal the answers to life, or teenage boredom. Melissa tilted the can, and for no particular reason, tipped some of its contents into the sink. She watched as the brown fluid, scattered with dots of air, traced its way towards the drain to drip slowly into oblivion.

Melissa was suddenly hit with fear. She felt that she would suddenly sink into a black void if she didn't do something exciting; or at least something adult, something that made her feel less of a kid. In an instant she dropped the soft drink can, so it spun and then fell on its side; foaming liquid gushed from its opening like the thoughts that had flooded her mind. She spun on her heel and marched towards the sofa. With a force that shocked Toby, Melissa yanked on his arm. The purpose of her action forced the boy to stand, and then follow, as Melissa strode towards the hall.

'Hey…what the fuck Mel!' Cried Toby. He twisted his neck to look at the television screen.

'Come with me,' replied Melissa, '…and don't say anything stupid.'

Melissa opened her bedroom door, more in anger and frustration than any sort of emotional need; she shut it with just as much force.

8

Gordon Andrews knelt on the manicured lawn and brushed leaves and small twigs from the base of the headstone. The grass was damp and he could feel the moisture touch the skin of the knee that had contacted the ground; it had passed slowly through the wool of his suit pants, undetected until it was too late to do anything about it. A walking stick steadied his aged body, he clasped it with both hands, genuflected, with his face against the curved handle. Slowly he removed some wilted flowers from a crystal vase that he had placed beneath the gold script many years ago. He paused for a moment and then turned to remove tissue paper from the stems of the roses he had bought from the florist.

For the first years after Celia had passed away, he had cut the roses from the ones she had cared for in their own garden, but the house had become too difficult to live in; a painful reminder of a tragic end, so he had sold the property he had once cherished. A small flat, and then a retirement village had only brought a numbness to a life that had been perpetually busy. The bookstore had been his salvation, not quite born-again, but invigorated to the point where he could embrace what he had, and placate what he had lost.

In silence, Gordon said a prayer, or was it a confession; a murmur of things that he was sorry for, things that he wished he could have changed, or controlled. He knew of course that he could not. Emma had appeared and he had fallen in love with her. It had struck him without warning. He had not fantasied or searched for something outside of his life with Celia and the university. The emotion of attraction to someone, the sudden need to have—what you didn't know existed—had hit Gordon hard. It had changed him, and then it altered the lives of those around him.

Gordon closed his eyes, an image of Thomas in uniform filled his mind. His son stood in the garden, by the roses, proud and self-assured, ready to meet the challenge ahead; his younger brother Jonathon, gazed in awe through the camera's eye-piece and then took the shot.

With purpose, Gordon pulled himself to his feet and gave one last look at his wife's headstone, he wanted to evade the image that always came next. It was an image shrouded in fog on a cold dock. The man was in uniform. He had shaken his hand and said, '*Hello Dad*,' but Gordon had been left dumb. The photo Jonathon had taken had sat on the mantle of the fireplace the entire time that Thomas was overseas. Each letter had been read beside it, and many brandies had been lifted towards it when there was nothing but the flicker of flames to light a dark night. But the man who stood in front of Gordon on the dock was not Thomas. His kit-bag said he was, but the sunken cheeks and the darkened eyes introduced someone else, someone moulded by battle and the screams of wounded men on a British island in the South Atlantic.

As he walked towards the bus stop Gordon promised himself that he would telephone Jonathon. He questioned himself about the time difference in Canada. It was a momentary diversion from the fact that the call would not be welcomed, or greeted with enthusiasm. He would call nonetheless, they could talk about Alex, a common source of pride.

**

Karen stubbed her cigarette out like she had tried to kill an insect. She jabbed and jabbed with her finger until it had made the glass ash-tray jump across the dining room table. She let go of the cigarette and then pushed hard on her forehead with the same hand to reduce her anxiety.

'Shit,' she muttered. 'Shit.'

She began to cry and then stopped the emotion abruptly. It caused her to inhale and then hold her breath momentarily before she exhaled.

'I can't fucking believe this,' she said in a whisper.

A thousand thoughts and images raced through her mind. They tortured her as no other parenting moment had; her coffee-date with Alex, its relaxed and sophisticated nature, now seemed like a dream.

She could hear her own screams, and then unexpectedly she laughed, sorrowfully, half-heartedly. The image of Toby as he had run across the lounge-room clutching a bed sheet with one hand and his clothes with the other, made her think of her youth.

I wasn't this young, she said to herself. *Why now, when Brad is away?*

Karen had known this day would come, but she still hadn't wanted it to, and she definitely hadn't wanted to walk in on it. Her chest tightened as her thoughts left the comical image of Toby and rested at the feet of hers and Melissa's heated, and physical, argument.

She had been shocked at what she had discovered; flustered, and then for some reason angry when she should have been calm.

Like any other day, Karen had opened the door while she juggled her keys, and whatever else she held; it didn't seem to matter if it was a lot or next-to-nothing. She had kicked off her shoes and revelled at the niceness that had stayed with her from the coffee shop, ready to enjoy a quite home while Mel was at school.

She had poured herself a glass of water from a bottle in the fridge when the strangest of noises had registered with her. Almost in a trance she had walked in search of its source and traced it down the hall. She still couldn't say why she opened the door, she just did, and then the rest was just a sequence of blurred images.

Karen asked herself why she had acted with such anger, and then fired a reply back to herself *because she's fucking sixteen, you idiot.* She suddenly felt, once again, where her palm had burned like fire after she had slapped her daughter on the face.

Karen had screamed, ridiculously, *what the fuck are you doing*, and then *get out of my house*. Mel had frantically wrapped herself in a sheet and then leapt to her boyfriend's defence. She had called her mother an *old hag*,' after Toby had sprinted from the room. Karen had reacted in anger and at the lack of respect shown to her by her daughter, but it was no excuse; she had never struck her daughter, or anyone, before that moment.

Karen remembered the expression of shock on Mel's face; the distortion in features that had changed defiant teenager to vulnerable child, as Karen stood before her confused and crazed.

She remembered how she had felt guilt and then repulsion towards her actions, as the fire inside of her had quelled. Karen had then turned and left her daughter alone and humiliated.

After that, she had walked in a daze to sit on the sofa. She cried again, but this time without restraint. 'What just happened?' She asked in complete frustration.

You hit your daughter, stated a voice inside her head. *Why?* The words came slowly and seemed to echo off the inside of her skull. They resonated with an intent that tore at her sole.

**

The sound of an idling engine had woken Karen from her half-sleep. She had curled up on the sofa, still in the clothes she had worn to the airport that morning. She heard a car door slam and sat bolt upright. She looked instinctively towards her hand where she still clutched her mobile phone, it hadn't left her since she had started ringing her daughter.

11.43pm.

There had been no answer, not to call or text. Karen had kept playing over in her mind, the scene where Melissa had stormed out, dressed in a hotchpotch arrangement of clothing, her rainbow patterned hessian bag clutched hard to her side.

Like so many things that afternoon and evening, Karen couldn't answer why she hadn't chased after Melissa. She still looked at her as her little girl and thought she would be back not long after the sun went down, but if she was honest, she would have admitted that she wanted to avoid another confrontation.

Karen rubbed her eyes and slid her phone into the pocket of her pants. She hadn't bothered to put shoes on as she rushed for the front door and the stairs that led to the ground floor entrance. The cold night air bit into her face as she opened the glass doors framed in timber, and her knees buckled when one foot hit a stone on the rough pavement.

Her heart stopped when she saw the police car; a uniformed officer stood outside, while another sat behind the steering wheel. He held a two-way microphone to his mouth.

'Melissa,' gasped Karen.

The police officer turned at the sound of Karen's voice.

9

Sydney, Australia

The carousel carried suitcases at a pace that hypnotised each of the tired and dehydrated passengers that had jostled for positions alongside the conveyor belt. Bradley rubbed his eyes again and then his neck, he didn't know how to describe it, but he felt like he had been covered in something. The view of Sydney Harbour from the plane's window, dancing under the setting sun, had lifted his spirits, but now all he could think of was a hot shower and some fresh clothes.

Finally, he spotted his battered black suitcase. He moved closer to the carousel determined not to let it slip by him; his fatigued mind and body could not endure another orbit.

Bradley claimed his baggage and then took a mint from his pocket and popped it in his mouth, it was the only thing he could think of to freshen himself up before he met his sister. He walked around the wall that opened to the public concourse, all at once seeing a mass of wide-eyed people ready to greet a friend or family member.

Gabi had spotted Bradley first, her eyes matched the enthusiastic, yet dignified wave that greeted the weary traveller from behind the balustrade. Gabi stood with an elegance that allowed only the barest of clues to her ambition and determination to succeed. To the casual observer she looked like the typical well-dressed wife of a wealthy

Vaucluse banker. They would be right about one thing, she was well-dressed, but she had never been married, nor was ever likely to be. She lived in Double Bay, and had made her own money.

'Hello little brother.'

'Good to see you Gabi.' Bradley leaned over the rail to give his sister a hug.

'Oh,' sighed Gabi, 'you have been on a plane full of people.'

'That bad is it? Would you believe me if I said I feel worse than I smell?'

'No,' replied Gabi bluntly, but with a smile. She pointed her finger politely towards the exit. 'My driver's waiting.'

'Sorry,' said Bradley, he walked with purpose along with other weary passengers.

Bradley and Gabi reunited at the end of the waist high partition, where the crowd had begun to disperse. They linked arms and headed for the exit.

'You travel light,' remarked Gabi.

Bradley shrugged his shoulders to suggest that not a lot of thought had gone into it. Gabi suddenly remembered why he was there and squeezed his arm a little tighter.

'It's good to see you Brad...he had a good life. I know it is an odd thing to say, but try not to weigh yourself down with regret.' Gabi began to walk and dragged her brother with her. In her own mind she acknowledged that her advice to Bradley had sounded indifferent, but she had cried enough in the last forty-eight hours to look at their father's passing more clearly.

Bradley didn't reply. He agreed it was an odd thing to say, from anyone else but his sister; she had always been direct, so he would not have expected anything else. She knew as well as Bradley that a typical father-son bond had not existed between Bradley and Dr Robert Johnson.

The automatic doors parted and Bradley was hit with the heat of an Australian summer. He sighed.

'A little warmer than Mother England,' said Gabi.

'Just slightly, you can never really appreciate it until you feel it again,' replied Bradley. 'What time is it?'

'8am. This is mild, I was in Adelong last week,' Gabi motioned to her left. 'We are this way.' She pulled out a mobile phone with a lid that flipped up; Bradley hadn't seen one before. He looked at his sister as she quickly typed a message; she radiated confidence and class, things he felt he lacked. She was forty-seven, but could pass for thirty-seven. Gabi had finished her law degree at Cambridge and then excelled, he had not. He thought about the place she had mentioned, it was a name he hadn't heard in a while. Gabi looked up at Bradley. 'On his way.'

Bradley looked at her hand.

'Oh, cute isn't it, I just picked it up today…apparently it's the latest and greatest in mobile phones.'

'You mentioned Adelong,' said Bradley tentatively, as they walked past a line of taxis and into an area that had hire-cars written on the road in bright yellow.

'Oh yes, the heat was ghastly…this is nothing. I went down to make sure of the funeral arrangements, and also pay a visit to our Uncle Jim and Aunty Mary.' Gabi waved her arm above her head and Bradley noticed a sleek black car, as it approached them.

'How is Jim?' Asked Bradley politely. He remembered the last time he had seen him, ten years ago. It had only been a brief reunion, but he recalled how intimidated he had felt. Jim was a nice person, but from a different time, and a different life to Bradley. He had found he had very little in common with the successful cattle-man and had struggled to strike up any lasting conversation. What Bradley hadn't realised, was that Jim was quiet, and over the years had allowed his actions to speak for him, making him a well-respected member of his community.

'Fabulous…Jim and his family have done so well for themselves. They got into Angus in a big way before anyone else knew what was going on. The Japanese cannot get enough of it apparently.' Gabi took a pace back as her car pulled up.

Bradley stared at her, as a tall fit-looking man in his twenties emerged from the driver side. He walked calmly, but with a respectable degree of urgency to open the rear door.

'It is a breed of cattle, darling, not whatever it is your rural-adverse mind is thinking.'

Bradley gave a relaxed smile. His sister was right, he never had understood his relatives' background. After all he had been raised in Cambridge, so had Gabi, but she had spent a lot of time in Adelong before Bradley was even born, or old enough to remember what it was like there. She seemed to be at ease in the country, or anywhere for that matter.

He remembered Gabi's stories of Adelong when they were children. He would curl up in his big sister's bed on cold Cambridge nights and listen intently, not because he dreamed to farm in rural Australia, but just to be by her side and away from the imaginary noises he would hear in the solitude of his own room.

'I will take that for you Mr Johnson,' said the burly chauffeur in a thick Aussie accent.

Bradley didn't reply.

'Thank you, Justin,' interjected Gabi, 'I think my brother has a severe bout of jet-lag, or lack of manners.'

Justin smiled at his boss and then closed the door gently behind them. He liked his job, so he always politely agreed with Gabi; she paid well and gave him plenty of time off to surf at his home-break of Manly, or anywhere else along the Northern Beaches of Sydney.

**

Bradley looked out the tinted windows, as he allowed his hand to caress the fine leather of his sister's luxury sedan. He stared at the sky-scrapers that sparkled in a way that made one feel energised, regardless of the twenty-three-hour flight they had endured. Bradley was glad to be in Gabi's presence, comforted in a way, and free from the tension that seemed to always lay over him at home.

'I have booked you and Robert in at the ANA...'

'I thought we would be staying with you,' replied Bradley, as he sat a little straighter. A part of him thought of the purse-strings, but another part had also wanted the company, especially if things got tense with his brother.

'You will,' replied Gabi, with the patience of an older sibling, 'but I thought you may like to take in some harbour views and your brother's company before the funeral...and besides I have a friend staying.'

'Oh…yes of course Gabi.' Bradley relaxed in his seat again. He thought about Gabi's friend, he wondered if it was the same one. He found it strange that for all his sister's confidence, strength of character, and success as a partner in a prestigious Sydney law firm, that she still referred to her lovers as friends. Why not call her by her name, or just say 'girlfriend'; they all knew, and always had, even their father. Maybe he had also tainted Gabi with his firmness and overbearing sense of right, as he had his two sons. Maybe it was society, or her work colleagues' need to present a certain picture. Whatever it was, he didn't understand the charade.

Bradley had always found it funny that while his visits to Australia exhilarated him, they were marked by a sense that he had stepped back in time, in terms of cultural and social acceptance. The twenty-four-hour flight, wiping two decades away.

'And don't worry, I will pick up the bill…just go easy on the bar-fridge.' Added Gabi.

'Ha,' Bradley turned quickly, like he had dozed off and then suddenly woken. 'That is very kind of you Gabi.'

Gabi flipped open her phone again and then closed it just as quickly. She looked out the window with a blank stare, and then turned her attention to her brother.

'Sorry Brad, I haven't asked how Karen and Melissa are…all well?' Gabi retrieved lipstick and a circular disc that opened as a mirror. She applied the lipstick as Bradley shrugged.

'Good…' Bradleys voice trailed off and Gabi raised an eyebrow.

'Really, that sounded chipper…is everything okay?'

'Yes, fine…you know what it's like,' replied Bradley, realising his sister probably didn't.

Gabi looked at Bradley. She couldn't help but be protective of him. She had always been like that, but more so since their mother died: he was the youngest.

She thought of Karen, although her sister in-law lived 17,000 kilometres away, she had never thought that her brother had the ideal marriage. He had more spark when he was younger and she had always thought of Karen as nice enough, but a bit of a wet-mop.

'Of course,' lied Gabi.

The sleek black sedan pulled up alongside the entry to the flash hotel. Bradley looked at the well-dressed porters and the shining fixtures that made up the façade. He looked back at Gabi, and like a child, he couldn't help but smile.

'Here we are…I won't escort you in.'

'Thanks again Gabi.'

'My pleasure, think of it as compensation for being a slack sister and not visiting you enough.' Gabi leaned over to kiss Bradley on the cheek. 'Have a shower…and we can meet up for lunch.'

'Sounds great.'

'I will call you,' added Gabi as Bradley stepped out of the limousine.

**

The staff had been friendly when Bradley had checked in; their politeness had gone to another level when they had glanced at the computer screen.

Gabi Johnson had some influence in Sydney-Town, Bradley had said to himself.

Bradley had gasped when he had opened the door to his room; suite was a better word. The view over Circular Quay and Sydney Harbour took his breath away. The vibrant colour that highlighted the activity on the beautiful blue waterway filled his heart with warmth and then a sudden sense of guilt at the enjoyment of such luxury in the absence of his wife, and in the lead up to his father's funeral.

He stood for a moment and took in the scenery. He felt strange at feeling undoubtedly at home in a place he didn't call home. Bradley always told himself that he was an Englishman, he was born in Australia, but he was English. The comfort that now ran through his veins suggested otherwise.

She would never move, he said to himself. A voice that lay even deeper admitted that neither would he.

Bradley swivelled on his heels in search of the bathroom. He found it and gave a quiet chuckle towards the opulence. A used towel reminded him of the inevitable reunion with his brother Robert. He ran the hot water and tried to think of something else.

**

Robert Johnson hit the punching bag with intent. He had settled into the luxurious hotel well but not with the same appreciation one might expect. Robert held a resentment towards wealth, not because he didn't like what it could bring, but because during his life it had evaded him.

The middle child of Dr Robert Johnson had worked hard, but had never acquired the money that could enable him to relax. Along with his wife Jan, they had inherited her parents' Pub in Hunslet, just south of Leeds. But life in a Yorkshire Pub was not an easy existence in the 1990's, or at any time for that matter.

Robert and Jan had two sons, both in their twenties. Matthew worked at the pub and had a girlfriend, who he would probably marry if he could afford a place of his own. The youngest, Billy, had caused them no end of trouble as a teen, and he continued as he supposedly became an adult. Maybe it was part of the reason the punching bag had been dealt such a hiding, but Robert had been angry long before

Billy's delinquency; it probably stretched back to when his mother Emma had died a slow and painful death.

Robert stopped hitting the bag and then walked to a bench that he had laid his towel on. He wiped his face and then tore off the mits that were now sodden with his sweat. He walked past the reception that maintained the gym, sauna and health spa and nodded to the attractive blonde. She suggested that he *'enjoy the rest of his stay'*, somehow Robert got the impression from her mechanical smile that she didn't really give a fuck if he enjoyed his stay or not.

He stood patiently at the lift as the illuminated numbers descended to where he stood. An older man suddenly stood beside him and he acknowledged his presence with a polite grimace.

'Had your workout young man?' Asked the eighty-something gent.

'Done nowt really,' replied Robert, in the dialect he had adopted over time as well as to gain a semblance of acceptance in a parochial South Yorkshire.

The man tilted his head as he deciphered what Robert had said. 'Interesting accent.'

'Sorry,' replied Robert with a warmer smile. 'I forgot where I am.' Robert stuck out his hand for the stranger to shake, 'Robert Johnson, Australian born, Cambridge raised, residing in Yorkshire.'

'Well, that is a mixture,' replied the man as he shook Roberts hand, 'Roger Telford, Bathurst, 50th wedding anniversary. Thought I would try the sauna out, almost killed me.'

Robert laughed, he liked Roger instantly. He didn't expect to come across a 'no bullshit person' like him in a place like this.

'Fifty years Roger, you're a better man than me,' said Robert, although he had never imagined life without Jan at any point of his marriage. They stepped into an open lift, Robert feeling better than when he had entered an hour earlier.

**

Robert opened the door to the suite and then shut it just as quickly. The noise made Bradley take a sharp breath from his seat on the sofa. He held a note in his hand that a porter had delivered minutes earlier.

'You've arrived little brother,' announced Robert. He strode across the floor to stand in between the large windows and where Bradley sat on the sofa. Bradley stood, his action was awkward and tentative.

'Hello Robert,' said Bradley softly. He put out his hand and his older brother gripped it firmly.

'Robert?' He huffed, 'you sound like such a poof when you say that.' Why don't you call me Rob like everyone else?'

Bradley shrugged, *a poof, that's nice. I am so glad Gabi put us in the same room,* he said to himself. He hadn't thought about why he called Robert, Robert, he just did.

'When did you get in?' Asked Rob, as if he had never insulted his younger brother.

'About an hour ago.'

'Flight was shite…how long was your stopover?' Rob made his way to the cabinet that hid a fully stocked bar-fridge. He pulled out two cans of Fosters Lager.

'Only an hour or two.'

'Lucky prick,' replied Rob, as he offered a can to his brother. 'I'm still on England time.'

Bradley hesitated and then took it; he didn't want to be called a poof again so soon after the initial branding.

'I sat in Bangkok airport for ten fucking hours… torture.' Rob opened his beer and then stood by the window. 'What about this fucking view? Beats the shit out of Hunslet.'

'How is Jan…and the boys? I spoke to her on the phone.' Bradley had opened his beer as well, but had taken a smaller sip. As the amber fluid hit his stomach, he wished he would had opted for something else after the long flight, but that would have been impossible if he wanted to have any sort of re-connection with his brother.

'Jan's still moaning, and Matthew is working hard at Pub…and Billy is Billy.'

Bradley noted the Yorkshire habit of dropping articles in grammar. He had also seen his brother stiffen as he mentioned his youngest boys name. It made him think of Melissa and the note he had received, although any problems he and Karen had or were about to have with Melissa, paled into insignificance alongside the trials Rob and Jan had endured with Billy.

Ring ASAP about Melissa. Bradley recalled the note now scrunched in his pocket. *Surely, they could last a few days without me having to intervene,* Bradley said to himself. He became annoyed that Karen had rung him so early in his trip and suddenly felt glad that he was so far away.

Bradley felt something hit the side of his head. It was immediately followed by a voice that barked. He looked down and identified a t-shirt as the object that had offended, then the noise repeated itself.

'Bender! Have you gone deaf?' Asked Robert.

'Huh,' replied Bradley. He gave a startled look towards his brother.

'I asked how Karen and Melissa are and you sat there like a half-wit.'

'Oh, sorry. Probably jet-lag.'

'So, how are they?'

'Fine…good I suppose. They fight a bit.'

'Glad I don't have one…no offence,' added Robert, 'boys are hard enough.'

Bradley smiled to pretend he hadn't been offended, while Robert drained the rest of his Fosters.

'We're meeting Gab aren't we?' Added Rob.

'She said she would call,' replied Bradley. He decided he would telephone Karen later, before they met their sister.

10

Bradley read the menu but he wasn't taking it in. For all he knew the scrolled writing could have been in a foreign language; some of it actually was. As his eyes moved restlessly, the sounds of people that passed by and the sparkle of Sydney Harbour seemed to meld into one distracting force.

He caught the smell of sea water and he breathed a little deeper to allow it into his lungs. Strangely, he had suddenly smelt his office at the council in Cambridge, as if it had been trapped somewhere inside of him, the scent of sea water having dislodged it and then pushed it aside. Bradley rubbed his nose to make sure it had definitely gone.

Gabi looked sideways at her brother after his sudden movement without moving her head, just her eyes.

'Seen anything you like gentleman?' She asked.

They both made undistinguishable noises that conveyed their personality type.

'I know!' Suggested Gabi. 'How long has it been since you have had lobster?'

Bradley looked up from his menu and thought seriously about his sister's question. Rob didn't move except for one of his eyebrows, which raised when he had located the price of the crustacean that his sister had mentioned on the menu.

'Just last week Gabrielle, plucked one out of River Aire I did,' said Rob. He exaggerated the Yorkshire in his accent and then smirked. Gabi smirked back. She hated it when Rob extended her name. She thought of her dad, and then fought off the emotion that threatened to unsettle her.

'Couldn't tell you,' replied Bradley.

Gabi composed herself. 'Well it is time you re-acquainted yourselves, my treat. I will have the grilled Whiting…I actually did have a lobster last week.' Gabi smirked once more for Rob.

'Thank you, Gabi,' said Bradley.

Rob snapped his menu shut and then leaned back on his chair to get the attention of the waiter. He held his empty beer bottle up for the restaurant employee to see.

'Yeh thanks Gab,' added Rob.

'My pleasure.'

Gabi placed her menu to one side. The waiter walked to the table and Gabi relayed what they would have and then turned her attention back to her brothers.

'A while back, when dad got sick, he told me that if he couldn't be buried near Mum, he would like to be buried in Adelong.' Gabi paused, and looked out over the harbour. She was glad that she had worn sunglasses, even when she was young, she had not liked to show her brothers when she was upset.

'Anyway, Dad was not really the sentimental type, but he said he felt Mum was in Adelong…in spirit I suppose, but he didn't say it that way. He said he would rather be buried in the country than the city.'

Bradley nodded in agreeance.

'Does it matter,' said Rob. 'I mean, we all end up dirt one way or the other.'

Gabi breathed in and held it for a moment. She decided not to reply to her brother's comment. 'I have made all the arrangements and we will leave the day after tomorrow.' Gabi paused as if she had forgot something, but she had just needed a moment to compose herself. An image of her mother's headstone had flashed before her eyes as it did every time she drove past a cemetery, or entered a church.

A platter of oysters, prepared in several different ways, and surrounded by small crusts of bread, was placed in the centre of the table by a discerning waiter. The arrival of the entrees that she had taken the liberty of ordering had been welcomed and allowed her to refocus on her brothers.

'Ah the oysters!' Exclaimed Gabi. They are my weakness boys, do try some…there is mornay, natural of course, kilpatrick, and watch the ones with the dollop of green. It's wasabi.'

Rob immediately picked up an oyster covered in Wasabi. He was compelled to; his sister had basically taunted him. Gabi glowed internally, happy that some things never change, even after you have realised that both your mother and father are now dead. You don't have parents anymore, but you still have family.

The middle, and probably most obstinate, Johnson child stared smugly at his older sibling, proud that once again he had shown her that she could not tell him what to do. Gabi picked up an oyster, without any condiment, and squeezed some lemon on it. She watched Robert's eye twitch; he placed the back of his hand on his mouth and then lent back in his chair. He tried to keep his composure by turning his head away from the table like he was a considerate smoker that didn't want to infect his table with the repugnant plume. Quickly he reached for his beer and took a large mouthful. Tears were in his eyes.

'Are you okay Rob?' Asked Bradley.

Gabi picked up two pieces of the bread that surrounded the oysters.

'Eat these.'

Rob grabbed the bread and stuffed it in his mouth like he hadn't eaten in a week.

'I told you to be careful Robert,' said Gabi.

Rob glared angrily at his sister, knowing she had asserted her authority without really having to do anything.

'Try the mornay Brad,' added Gabi, before taking a sip of her wine, 'you won't find better anywhere in the world.'

**

The afternoon had gone pleasantly; Rob had gotten over his wounded pride and Bradley had relaxed after a couple of glasses of wine. The Johnsons had shared desserts and caught up on each other's lives and the details of their father's funeral. They were to meet the solicitor for the reading of the will at 9am the next day. The men had listened intently as Gabi relayed what she had achieved in her professional life. Rob had even hidden his usual sarcasm or faintly disguised bitterness that came with someone else's achievement and the acquisition of wealth. Bradley had felt embarrassed of how little he knew of his sister's accomplishments.

Roused by his sister, Bradley raised his glass.

'To Dad.' The toast came out awkward and there was a brief pause. Bradley felt awkward at the fact that he felt awkward for toasting his own father.

'To Dad,' said Gabi. She smiled at her little brother. She never understood why their father had been so tough on him, so unwilling to be kind. Dr Robert Johnson had not always been like that. He had been a different man when his wife was alive, and Gabi felt fortunate that she was old enough to remember him then. She knew that was the image she had always held onto. She would always forgive her father for his stubbornness and hardening heart. It was these characteristics that seemed to grow as the distance between the present and the time he spent with the love of his life became greater.

'To the old-man,' added Rob.

Bradley took a sip of his wine and then looked down into his lap. His mind replayed a scene that seemed to invade his thoughts from time-to-time, usually when he was feeling despondent or he allowed himself to think of what might have been. He was standing in front of his father who was seated in an armchair at his apartment in Cambridge; the one he used when visiting from Australia.

'It doesn't surprise me...have you ever stuck at anything?'

He had just told his father that he wanted to drop-out of law. It wasn't such an unusual scene; Bradley was certain that fathers and sons had those sorts of conversations all the time. If his father had yelled at him or somehow got upset, it may not have been so damning, but Dr Johnson had remained calm—disconnected. He had said what he had said, looked down towards the glass he held and swirled the brandy inside it.

'Your mother would be proud,' he had added before downing the brandy. He then stood and left the room to be alone in his study.

Bradley clenched his teeth as he sat in the restaurant in Sydney's eastern suburbs. He let out a sob and a trickle of mucus was forced from his nostril. He reached for his trouser pocket and pulled out a handkerchief. He frantically wiped his nose and then put his thumb and forefinger to his eyes. Gabi gave her youngest brother a look of concern and then reached out to touch his arm.

'Why did he dislike me so much?' Asked Bradley.

'Brad,' sighed Gabi.

'I mean, I know that he thought I wasn't up to his standards…wasn't good enough. But why didn't he like me?'

'Because he was an old prick,' interjected Rob.

'Rob,' hissed Gabi.

'Well he was.' Rob took a mouthful of his beer and fell into silence.

Gabi pulled her chair closer to Bradley's. She leaned over and kissed his forehead in a motherly way, not knowing—for the time being—the exact right thing to say. She had a sip of her own wine.

'I don't know why Dad was the way he was with you Brad…or you Robert,' Gabi glared at Rob as she spoke. 'All I can say that he wasn't always like that. You may or may not remember, but he was never the same after Mum died, how could he be?' Gabi looked over the water to gather her thoughts. 'I guess, we were never the same…Mum suffered greatly and Dad suffered with her. I can remember on many nights cooking dinner for us while Dad was at the hospital with Mum.'

Gabi looked over at Rob. He was staring at his beer bottle, twisting it in the palm of his hand, as if the label had captivated him, but she knew he was listening.

'I would hear him come home at God knows what hour, sometimes he would eat the food I had left him, most of the time I found him asleep on the sofa,' said Gabi.

'But…'

'I don't know Bradley,' interjected Gabi. She turned to Rob. 'I don't know why he was the way he was with you boys. We had our fights and disagreements, but I am not silly enough to suggest to either of you that our individual relationships with Dad were anything close to being the same.'

'You're a lawyer Gabi, you made it,' said Rob. He said it quietly, but the bitterness was there. Gabi didn't let the barb affect her.

'Let me get the bill and we can go back to your hotel for a coffee,' said Gabi.

'Sorry Gabi, this isn't your fault,' said Bradley.

'It's okay Brad, we need to do this…we need to talk.'

**

The cab ride back to the hotel had been mostly in silence, even the chatty Greek driver had eventually caught the mood and ceased with his story about his father's fishing boat in a village near Kalamata. Bradley had not known the name of the village; the word Kalamata had only stuck because it reminded him of the olives; the ones Melissa always picked from pizzas.

As the lift rose, the numbers illuminated and then didn't, to prove they were in fact moving, Bradley thought of the Greek man, or was that wrong to say Greek. Barbara at the council would have corrected him and said Greek-Australian, but Bradley appeased himself with the knowledge that in general Australians were not concerned with such sensitivities, and the cab driver would have probably been grateful not to be called something else, like wog or dago.

'He seemed like a nice person,' said Bradley.

Rob pulled a face like a bad smell had suddenly invaded the lift. 'What...who is nice?'

Bradley smiled as he remembered the cab driver. The man had obviously developed a habit over the years that saw him roll his hand forward while he spoke. Even in the confined space of his taxi his trait had continued unabated while he spoke to the Johnsons. Sometimes slow, others quicker, but always with the tempo of his voice. The conversation hadn't lasted long; the Johnsons and their indifference had made sure of that, but Bradley had watched him and now he remembered the man's efforts and the fact that he was undoubtedly happy.

'The taxi driver, he was a jovial fellow…happy.'

A bell chimed and the lift door opened. Rob stepped straight into the corridor.

'How the fuck should I know Brad.'

Gabi held out her arm to suggest that her youngest brother should step out of the lift as well. She also gave him a warm smile that told Bradley not to worry about Rob's callousness. Gabi knew her brother well enough to know that the hardened exterior that had begun to form at the restaurant and then set like rock in the taxi, was just Rob's way of dealing with things that he would rather avoid.

Rob was first to the door of the suite. He had already inserted the plastic card into the slot when Bradley and Gabi caught up with him. As a reflex, he had also whined under his breath that he liked old fashioned keys better.

Aware of his own mood, Rob suddenly made an effort to be civil and held the door of the suite open for his brother and sister.

'After you.'

'Thank you, Rob,' said Gabi.

Bradley went to the cabinet that contained the bar fridge and began to look.

'I will call room service Brad,' said Gabi, 'it will be just as quick…and nicer.'

Gabi and Bradley were half way through their coffees before Gabi spoke. Rob had barely touched his.

'Have you thought what you will do with your inheritance?'

After the sound of her voice had died and the room had become silent again, Gabi acknowledged to herself that she could scarcely believe that she had said what she had said.

From the restaurant to the hotel, she had agonised over how she would broach the subject of her father's failed relationships with his sons. That is why she had practically ignored the friendly Greek taxi driver, she had been deep in thought, but she had resurfaced from deep-thought without any answers.

The sudden and direct question may have lacked tact, but it had the desired result.

'I hadn't thought about it…I mean, I had,' stuttered Bradley, 'I just concluded that I wouldn't …'

'Get anything,' interjected Rob.

Bradley shrugged his shoulders.

'Well, I can assure you…' Gabi stopped mid-sentence. 'I can't assure you actually, because I haven't seen Dad's will, but I am confident that you will…"get something", as you put so eloquently Rob.'

Gabi raised herself slightly from the soft lounge she sat in; just enough to grab one of the pastries that had come with the coffee.

'I shouldn't, but…'

The eldest Johnson savoured the sweetness before she spoke.

'As I said at the restaurant, I cannot explain why our father was so cold towards you boys.' Gabi caught her choice of words and their maternal connotations, but both Rob and Brad had been boys when their father's attitude had turned, so in a way a part of them had been trapped in that period, forever adolescent; at least in regards to Robert Johnson senior.

'It is something that I sincerely hope that you will come to deal with in time. But, without wanting to sound crude, you will be decidedly more comfortable financially, after we meet with dad's solicitor tomorrow.'

Gabi took another sip of her coffee to formally announce that she had finished. It wasn't how she imagined it. She gathered most people would have just sat around and eventually told loving stories or quirky personal memories of the person that had passed, like people had when her mother had died. The other business would just take care of itself.

Bradley allowed Gabi's comments to swim around in his head for a while, as he tried to determine exactly what they meant. Rob stayed silent like Bradley, but Gabi's words would not float in his mind for long, there were far too many other thoughts that collided with the ones his big sister had introduced.

Where Bradleys mind was a lake, calmed by the weight of thought, Rob's had become a storm; the sudden influx of information too much to prevent a release of pent-up emotion. The coffee and assorted pastries sat on a silver tray that rested on a lacquered timber table. Rob picked it all up and then flung it across the tiled floor that was the suite's foyer.

11

Cambridge

Karen brought two mugs of hot chocolate from the kitchen to the lounge room. Melissa sat with a blanket wrapped around her body. Her legs were tucked up and to the side to escape the cold that was never entirely pushed out of their unit by the gas heater.

Melissa had not been back to school since the police had dropped her home. It had been Karen's idea; just as much for herself, as her daughter. She had needed time to think, and she had got just that; Melissa had not uttered a word for the first eighteen hours.

When Bradley had called and asked what the problem was, she had paused before she spoke. *How could I explain what happened without starting a whole new argument*, she had asked herself. Bradley was on the other side of the world, Melissa was safe, and it could wait until he got back. She made up a story about how she wished she had said goodbye properly at the airport, and she just wanted to speak to him. She felt shitty for making the story up, but nice for saying something pleasant, instead of what they had been used to of late.

'There you go, one hot chocolate…a marshmallow too.'

'Thanks.'

'Anything on?' Asked Karen.

Melissa blew on her hot drink and then looked down at the television guide that sat in her lap.

'Not much...*Four Weddings and a Funeral.*'

'Oh, that's not bad...we can watch that.'

'Sure,' replied Melissa without enthusiasm.

'Or, whatever you want Mel.'

Karen sipped her hot chocolate. She didn't want to ruin the moment. She had made progress since lunch time that day. A stilted talk, some anger and accusations that had led to tears, and then finally a sense of connection. The absence of her husband had forced Karen to confront something that she should have long ago; she had drifted from her only child.

At first Karen had found it hard. She had said sorry easily enough, because she truly was. The way she had reacted in her daughter's bedroom had been more about herself than Melissa. The acknowledgment of her own pent-up feelings made her feel worse. Although Karen knew it deep down her reaction had allowed it to escape. Her life was tainted by regret and not making the most of things, and instead of fighting she had allowed those emotions to consume her.

What she had found hard, was confronting her emotions, and not imposing her own insecurities on her daughter; not transferring the fear that had guided each move and decision she had made into the only thing of importance she had created. She didn't want to say to her daughter, *enjoy these years, because it only gets tougher.* She wanted to say, *enjoy these years and cherish them…and then make some more.* And she did, and her daughter hugged her, and they both cried. Karen had also told Melissa that she loved her. A lump had formed well into her throat when she realised the length of time that had passed since she had last said it.

**

Mother and daughter sat side by side in a room that was dark except for the light from the television. Karen had let out little sounds at various times that sounded like a car going over a speed bump quickly. She had anticipated the parts in the movie that had made her laugh when she had gone to the cinema by herself to watch it. The smile that never left her face had nothing to do with the movie. It came from the warm glow that filled her body after having done the simplest, yet most difficult of tasks. She had opened herself up and it felt good: she hoped that Melissa had felt the same.

Melissa felt a similar warmth, but she had also checked her feelings with negative thoughts that did their best to sabotage the connection that had been made. She couldn't completely dispel the humiliation her mum had caused her, and she still wasn't sure about being struck; she felt bitterness, confusion and humility all at the same time in regards to her mum's actions. Part of her had said she had deserved it. If she had said something similar, or with the same intent to wound towards one of the toughies in the school yard, she may have received more than just an opened hand slap.

The teenager, who so desperately wanted to be seen as older than that, also remembered the fear she felt when she had found herself huddled under an overpass. Without Toby to lean on and unwilling to return home, she had decided to show how independent she was. By chance, a patrol car had passed by, stopped and made a U-turn to park in front of her before any harm had come.

The streets, darkened by night, only had life in the form of shadows or the headlights of cars that raced towards a destination. This Cambridge had a completely different feel to the one Melissa knew. It was the sounds that had chilled and then weakened her resolve the most. She remembered how they had made her eyes dart in different directions, and made her mind think of home. She had grunted at the police officer when he had asked her questions, but she had really wanted to hug him.

Melissa scooped the last of the frothed milk covered in chocolate from the bottom of her cup as she watched the movie with her mum. She enjoyed the homeliness of it, even though it was cold and really not all that enjoyable. She showed herself that she was sincere in her efforts to be agreeable when she pushed those negative thoughts to one side. She would steal a glance in her mother's direction each time she had made her strange sound. Melissa would smirk, not at what had transpired in the film, but what she saw as her mum's goofiness; so nice, and so removed from her mother's detachment or anger that had seemed to constantly simmer, like an overcooked meal in a forgotten about pot.

**

Gordon looked down at the electric bar heater from his seat in front of the antique desk, to see if it was actually turned on. The element glowed bright red, but the heat didn't seem to transfer much further than his aching knees.

The only other source of warmth in his shop were two portable oil heaters, and they didn't seem to make a difference either. He decided then and there to invest in the gas heating his granddaughter had suggested instead of fighting the cold and damp Cambridge winter days. Alex had told him it would be better for the books anyway. She seemed to know something about everything at the tender age of twenty-one: Gordon thought of his granddaughter's confidence and smiled.

He rubbed his spindly legs, momentarily remembering the muscle that was once there. He glanced at the package to his left, neatly wrapped in brown paper. He was certain that Bradley would have been in to pick up his book by now, but he hadn't, and Gordon returned his attention to cataloguing a pile of ten books.

Above him, but slightly to the rear, the creak of timber and then the faintest of footsteps told him Alex had risen from bed. She would shuffle around for a moment and then eventually bring her grandfather a mug of hot tea. More often than not, she would sit in silence and allow the warmth of her drink to kick-start her body, only speaking if absolutely necessary.

When she had finished, she would retreat upstairs, shower and change. Her second appearance down the stairs and into the bookstore would reveal an almost completely different person; the energetic and bright-eyed girl that people knew as Alex.

Alex glanced around the bookshop in one sweeping motion, like she was acknowledging her transformation. 'Where would you like me to start,' she asked.

Gordon swivelled on his chair and stared at Alex.

'Why don't you put the same stuff in my tea that you put in yours?'

'Very funny grandpa, you know I need a moment in the morning to get started.'

'Well, if you want to help, you can go through that box of books just behind me. Be ruthless though, the order of my chaos has started to get out of hand.'

'Ruthless it is,' replied Alex.

The antique bookstore owner and his granddaughter worked in silence for five minutes, before Alex suddenly stood and headed for the kitchenette at the rear of the store.

'Another cup of tea?' She yelled, when half way down an aisle.

'Why not,' replied Gordon.

Moments later, Alex returned with two mugs of tea. The mugs being something that Alex had gradually introduced to her grandfather's life; he had always used china cups before her arrival in England.

Gordon took a tentative sip to test the contents temperature and then invited Alex to sit. She looked around for a second and then decided to lean with her back to her grandpa's antique desk.

'I spoke to your father yesterday.'

Alex didn't respond. Instead, she took a sip of her own tea, and then waited for what was to follow. Her father and grandfather didn't talk all that much. They didn't necessarily fight, but she was well aware and increasingly embarrassed by her father's impatience with his father.

'He was well,' stated Gordon. 'He asked how you were...I told him that I had never seen anyone work so hard in all my years at the university.' Gordon Andrews took a sip of his tea and then smiled at Alex. 'He didn't seem to buy it.'

'I should call,' said Alex. 'I did last week, now that I think about it...but then I suddenly realised that it was about four-thirty in the morning and I hung up.'

'Well, let me just say that I wasn't as alert as you,' replied Gordon. 'It was somewhere around the same time, but I didn't hang up.'

Alex laughed and then took another sip of her tea. Her mood changed into one of reflection. Gordon looked at her in silence. He assumed that his granddaughter was thinking about her parents, so he was shocked when she spoke.

'Tell me about that man's mother.'

Gordon's eyes squinted. He replayed Alex's sentence in his mind to make sure he hadn't missed something.

'Sorry, whose mother?'

'You know,' continued Alex, as if the subject should have been obvious from what she had said, 'the man that was in here the other day...oldish'

Gordon looked at her, still puzzled.

'...you were up the ladder and I shouted at you for being up there...that man.'

'Oh, of course, Bradley,' replied Gordon. He smiled for so many reasons.

'If you don't mind?' added Alex.

Gordon almost asked why she wanted to know about her, but he didn't. Instead, he asked himself what he would reveal. He took a sip of his tea and gathered his thoughts.

'Well she…sorry the lady's name was Emma…Emma Johnson.' Gordon covered his mouth with a clenched fist and forced a cough to clear his mind more so than his throat. Emma lectured at the university and that's how I came to know her. She came here from Australia…and I have to admit Alex, that up until that point, and in my own snobbish way, I thought the majority of Australians were oafish descendants of convicts.'

Gordon smiled at Alex to take the sting out of his comment, but it had some truth in it, and Alex realised that and admonished him accordingly.

'Grandpa! I know lots of lovely Aussies…that's so rude.'

'Name one,' replied Gordon, in jest.

Alex was stumped, so she turned to her original line of questioning. 'Were you and Emma friends?'

An image of a woman floated through Gordon's mind. Alex thought that her grandfather had answered her with his look, but it only raised further questions in her mind.

'Yes, we were friends. Work colleagues and friends, but she passed away some time ago…Emma had a wonderful mind and a fantastic energy that…she was very popular here.'

Alex nodded her head slowly in acceptance of her grandpa's statement. 'And now you know her son…small world.'

'Yes, it is Alex.' He drank the remainder of his tea and then stared at one of the many piles of used books. 'So small that you find your mistakes following you, but oddly big enough that any triumphs seem to vanish as quickly as they appeared.'

'Sorry grandpa?'

Gordon suddenly appeared more alert. He had allowed his most closely held thoughts to escape. 'Never mind Alex, just the ramblings of an old man…a poor attempt at being philosophical.'

Alex looked at her grandfather. Her curiosity was aroused by concern, but the concern was enough to evoke cautiousness. She decided to let sleeping dogs lie.

12

Adelong, Australia

Bradley smiled politely at the bar attendant, picked up his beer, and then moved hesitantly into the small crowd that had gathered for his father's wake at the Adelong Services Club in rural New South Wales. He didn't really want the drink, but it had been a way of occupying himself while he figured out what to say to the next person who offered their hand to shake. *Thank you for coming*, had been his default phrase; Gabi was doing better; floating from one person to the other as if she resided in the small country town all her life.

He continued to look at his older sister, not noticing Rob move up alongside him.

'Don't feel bad little brother,' said Rob before downing the remainder of his beer. He wiped his mouth with his thumb and forefinger. 'She's a lawyer, she talks bullshit every day.'

Bradley took a sideways glance at Rob.

'What?'

Bradley let Rob suffer for a moment. 'Do you know any of these people?'

'Except for Uncle Jim, Aunty Mary and the boys, nought…they seem to know us.' Rob tapped the side of his empty glass. 'I'm getting a beer, meet me over at the snooker table.'

Brad nodded. *It will pass the time*, he thought. As he walked, Brad looked around at various things hanging on the wall, without really taking note of anything. A hand was placed on his shoulder, and he turned to see an elderly gentleman with his hand outstretched.

'Terribly sorry to hear about your father young Rob.'

'Bradley.'

'Sorry, Brad, yes of course…Roger Harding. He was a good man, your father, and the best GP we've ever had. The elderly man sneaked a quick glance around the room. 'I hope doc Fields didn't hear me say that, he might cut my blood-pressure pills off. The old man placed his hand on Bradley's shoulder and allowed his head to dip, as he laughed at his own joke. Bradley smiled, and realised it was probably the first time he had all day.

'Anyway, young fellow I won't keep you, I was headed to the men's myself, but I saw you and had to say hello.' Roger held out his hand again, and Bradley shook it gently. Roger placed his left hand over the top of his and Bradley's. 'You know, the last time I saw you was right across the street with your mum…funny how you suddenly remember things.'

Bradley raised his eyebrows and gave a forced smile. Roger patted him on the shoulder again, and walked slowly away. Bradley looked out the glass doors in a vain attempt to see the main street. He tried to manufacture an image of his mother, young, and with a toddler: nothing came to him. He walked towards the snooker table where Rob was busy chalking a cue.

'I'll break seeing as you took so long,' said Rob

'Sure,' replied Bradley. He knew Rob's unreasonable assertiveness was his way of dealing with what was going on. Agreeing with him was the easiest way of getting through the day.

Brad's thoughts drifted back to his conversation with Roger. He looked out the window at the end of the room. He tried to manufacture an image of his mother. The best he could do was a lady in a dress with her backed turned. She bent down to wipe a little boy's cheeks with a small handkerchief. The little boy looked straight at him.

'Rob?'

The elder brother stood from the position he had taken to line up his shot. 'Yeh.'

Brad cleared his throat. 'Do you think about mum?'

'Sometimes,' Rob shrugged to shake off how much he had understated his answer.

Brad didn't answer. He looked back out the window again, and his brother resumed his position at the snooker table.

Rob hit the white ball hard: more than one person turned their way after it crashed into the triangle of red. Rob watched a red ball roll close to the corner pocket, but it stopped short of going in. 'That's shite,' Rob pointed at the ball with his cue. 'Present for you Brad.'

Bradley moved slowly around the table to line up his shot, annoyed at himself that he expected reciprocation from his brother.

'Who was the old fella?' asked Rob, desperate to change the subject.

'Roger…he knew dad. A nice chap.'

'Chap?' Rob laughed 'You've got to come up to Hunslet one day…the boys at the bar would love you.' Rob pointed his cue towards his brother. 'Don't follow in with the white…no pressure.'

Bradley didn't look up from his cue. He made his shot, but he could see the ball veering slightly to the left from the moment he struck it. The cue-ball made contact with the red, but the angle made the ball ricochet off the cushion and out towards the centre of the table.

Rob laughed.

'Having fun?' asked Gabi, as she approached the table.

'I would be if we had made a bet on this game,' replied Rob.

Gabi looked at her brothers and tilted her head. She gave an exaggerated smile. 'Maybe you should mingle with some of the guests...just a thought.'

'Sure, Gabi,' said Bradley. He turned to the wall and placed his cue in the rack. Rob huffed.

'Come and have a chat to Tony and Mark...they're your cousins, and partners now.'

Bradley moved closer to his sister. 'They didn't seem too chatty before...are they okay with everything?'

'Perfectly,' said Gabi, in a business-like tone. 'Nothing has changed for them; dad was always a silent partner, unless you've decided to move?' Gabi winked at Bradley, and his mouth opened slightly. Gabi placed a placating hand on his forearm. 'Just stirring, let's not discuss that here.' She reached for Brad's hand, and squeezed it gently. 'You should talk to Tony; he has been telling me about our family history. I told him that you are very interested in that sort of thing.'

Gabi turned to look at Rob as she slipped her arm around her youngest brother's elbow. She noted the vacant and troubled look on his face: she longed for him to be content. 'You too Rob,' she said, as she led Bradley away.

**

Rob had lasted fifteen minutes with Gabi, Bradley and cousin Tony's revelations about their relative's wartime

127

feats, before he had casually slipped out a side door and onto a grassed area.

The Australian summer sun hit him like a blow torch, and he suddenly appreciated the small club's air-conditioning; still, he opted for the heat over education.

Gabi's throw-away line about Bradley moving had stirred something in him. He knew nothing of farming, but he had possessed about the same amount of knowledge in regards to pubs when he moved to Hunslet, and he had begrudgingly made a go of that. Farming would be tough; he had admitted to himself.

He started to think of the long Yorkshire winters, and he shivered under the intense southern hemisphere sun. He heard the door to the side of the club open.

Rob turned to see his cousin Mark, he held two beers in one hand by spreading his fingers while he gently closed the door with his other. Rob suddenly realised how big his cousin was.

'Thought you might like one of these,' said Mark. 'Tony is still talking.'

Rob smiled and then downed the beer he held in his hand with one mouthful. 'Thanks Mark.' He burped. 'Sorry Mark…beers a bit gassier than ours.'

Mark raised his eyebrows. 'Is that right…never been to England…like to, one day.'

'Not missing much Mark, but I suppose it's good for a visit.'

'Bet it's not as fuckin hot,' said Mark, before taking a big mouthful of beer.

Rob laughed, and realised he hadn't given his relatives a chance inside. He promised himself he would try to relax a bit more. 'No, you are right there, Mark...we don't really have a summer.' Rob had a mouthful of beer. 'The winters are something though.'

'Nice snow.'

'No, just fucking miserable.' Both men laughed hard.

'You just put up with it don't you, doesn't matter where you live,' said Mark.

'I suppose you do, mate.' Rob decided he liked Mark Mayfield. 'How's the farm?

'Not bad Rob, better than this time last year...at least there's a bit of feed about. We have a block up in the Gilmore Valley that is quite good actually...come to think of it, so do you.'

Rob shock his head instead of replying verbally, he didn't want to say something stupid.

'I can take you up there if you like...show you around.'

'Yeh, for sure, I'd love to have a look around,' replied Rob.

'Your old-man used to come down every now and then, and I'd take him for a spin…wasn't really his go though. Gabi gets into it when she gets the chance, you wouldn't pick it, lawyer and all.' Mark had a mouthful of beer. 'Handy to have one in the family, I say.'

Rob smiled at his cousin's joke. It was a strange feeling for Rob to hear Mark talk about his father. Rob was aware that he has made little or no effort to interact with his dad, but it still seemed odd to have gaps filled in by someone he barely knew. It was more comfortable for Rob to keep Dr Robert Johnson's life compact and simple. New pieces of information, adding new dimensions to his life, could threaten to introduce likeable elements to his character. Rob tried to shake from his mind the image of his father berating him in front of his mates.

'Could I get you another beer Mark,' asked Rob.

'That would be great Rob, I'll come inside with you and introduce you to a couple of blokes.'

13

Eight-year-old, Jack Mayfield, latched the gate to their property Skyview and then leapt into the back of the ute alongside two kelpies. He quickly rapped the roof of the Toyota Hilux twice. His younger brother, Tom, nudged his fathers' leg with his own, reminding the man in the driver's seat that Jack had signalled the okay.

Rob looked down at the young boy from the passenger seat and smiled. The wannabe farmer was dressed in jeans, leather boots and a blue cotton long sleeved shirt that was turned up at the cuffs.

'I think you are going to be a farmer like your dad, Tom,' said Rob.

Tom Mayfield looked up at the stranger sitting in the seat his brother normally occupied. He squinted his eyes slightly, having taken offence to Rob's statement. He couldn't get the words past his mouth, but as far as he was concerned, he was a farmer.

'A man of few words, our Tom,' offered Mark, as he drove slowly along a track and then through a shallow gully. Over the crest the ground was gently sloping, but with an area the size of two football fields that was basically flat. They drove around an old shearing shed that appeared to have not been used in some time, and then passed a set of new-looking cattle yards. 'Have a look down there Rob.'

Rob took his eyes from the corrugated iron shed, and looked through the windscreen of the four-wheel-drive. The brakes gave a slight squeak as Mark brought the vehicle to a complete stop; he whistled, and in a flash his two dogs had scrambled over the sideboard of the vehicle: Jack was only a second or two behind them.

'Not bad, hey,' stated Mark.

The view in front of Rob fell away into a sweeping valley, dotted by Eucalypts and lined with grass that had browned, but still held a tinge of green in the middle of summer. To the east, the hills were capped more densely with the native trees, and in the far-off distance, a haze gave a hint to part of the Snowy Mountains: Rob was awestruck.

'It's always a bit better up here…feed-wise,' added Mark.

The Yorkshire publican went to speak, but restrained himself with a certain alarm, when he felt a lump forming in his throat. He walked a few paces forward instead, and used the kelpies to disguise his emotion. He crouched down to pat them while he stared at the beautiful view. Mark let him be for a moment, for some reason he had sensed that Rob would appreciate it.

'Jack, take your brother and open that main yard, we'll run these heifers in.'

Jack ordered Tom to follow him, with the younger brother obeying, but he dragged his feet enough to show

Jack that he was not under his control. The kelpies scampered after the boys sensing something was a-foot; their departure roused Rob from his day dream, which made him turn towards Mark. He replied to his cousin's statement like no time had elapsed at all. 'Why is that?'

'Huh?'

'Why is there more feed up here,' asked Mark.

'Oh, a few reasons. Mainly it's just not quite as hot. We're not that far from our other properties, but it's just a bit more protected. It's good, because it gives us an option when the conditions are tougher…like they were over the last few years.'

Rob nodded. He took in the view again to clear his mind, he suddenly had questions to ask. He tried to start slowly, but sub-consciously the most pressing came out first. 'How come no one lives up here?'

'They did, once.' Mark asked Rob to follow him with a jerk of his head. The two men approached the yards and were met by Jack and Tom.

'Everything's ready Dad,' stated Jack. Tom nodded his agreeance.

'Thanks, boys. I am just going to show Rob something and then we will start.' Jack and Tom looked at each other for a moment, and then darted off towards the old shearing shed, having communicated something between each other with a simple look.

'Looks like they have something planned,' said Rob.

'God only knows,' replied Mark with obvious pride. 'This way Rob.' Mark led his cousin past the yards, and around behind the shearing shed. He casually looked right and saw his sons inspecting one of the timber piers. They had their faces centimetres from it; Jack was delicately prodding at the timber with his finger, and then turned to drop something in his brother's hand. *Termites*, thought Mark. He sighed, relieved to have discovered their harmless mission, but reminded that the shed would take a lot to repair, termites aside.

Rob followed Mark along the elevated paddock scattered with cow-pats. They turned as the face of the hill bent away from them, the valley to their left following. After a hundred metres or so the ground started to rise again, with a clump of Eucalypts partially obscuring what lay ahead.

As they came closer to the trees, Rob could see that they covered only twenty metres or so, and he was stunned to see a slightly run down, but still elegant homestead perched on top of the rise. It commanded a one hundred-and eighty-degree views of the valley below.

Rob stopped and looked back from where they had come. Although the climb had appeared gentle, he was now looking down on the roof of the shearing shed, and the valley, which he had so much admired before, seemed even more remarkable from where he now stood.

'My grandparents' home,' said Mark. He wiped his brow and took some deep breaths. 'I'm not very fit,' he added.

Rob breathed easily. He smiled at Mark, without comment on his cousin's lack of fitness. Unloading kegs of beer had helped keep him in reasonable condition, along with the occasional workout. 'No one lives here?'

'This is where my dad…and your mum lived for a bit, before they moved.'

'Can we go up?'

'Of course.' Mark glanced back at the shed and Rob saw it.

'Do you want to get the boys,' asked Rob.

'Na,' replied Mark exhaling, 'the shed will keep'em busy for a bit.'

Rob stared at the old shearing shed for a moment. He pictured his sons as youngsters. They stood in the lane that ran down the side of the pub with a tattered football. They would play in the little space they had, wrapped in jumpers and jackets to ward off the cold and damp Yorkshire winter. A hand wiped across a snotty nose was almost a reflex action for his kids, and he wondered how they would have grown up in a place like this. He also wondered for himself.

Mark held his arm out for Rob to lead the way. They came to a picket fence that had rotted in places and been trampled by ill-mannered cattle in others. A white tape, only a centimetre wide, was there in its place.

'Careful mate, it's hot,' said Mark.

'Huh?'

Mark pointed to the white tape. 'Electric fence.'

'Right,' replied Rob. He took an involuntary step back.

'It's got a decent kick.' Marked walked over to a red box, suspended high enough on a tree to be out of reach of the livestock. 'Good as gold now. Once upon a time, I would have let you touch it.' Mark slapped Rob on the back and walked towards the old homestead.

Rob walked slowly towards the house. He glanced back down the valley, before taking a tentative step onto the stairs that led to the verandah.

'They're pretty solid,' said Mark. 'Whole house is actually…just a couple of verandah posts and a skirting board here and there inside.'

Rob took in the view from the verandah. 'I can't believe no one lives here.'

Mark looked around the yard. He ran the ride-on mower over it every now and then; mainly to keep it a bit safer for the kids if they ventured up here, but also because a part of him was sentimental.

'Have a look at the fucking view! Stated Rob.

Mark shrugged and thought of ways to justify the wonderful homestead's neglect. 'It's easier near town…kids sport, shops.' The farmer hadn't convinced himself.

'You sound like my missus,' said Rob. He wished he hadn't. He suffered through the silence for a moment.

'Would you like to have a look inside?' asked Mark.

'Love to,' replied Rob. *No damage done,* he thought to himself.

'It was built in 1885, I think.' Mark took a key from an oddly placed shelf to the left of the front door. The door creaked as it was opened, and Rob smiled at how appropriate the sound was. 'It's a bit dusty, but feel free to look around. The room to your left was the lounge room. It was called the parlour on the original plans…I have them at home, framed. It was a gift from mum.'

Rob made eye contact with Mark to let him know that he was listening, but he was entranced by the old building and a force asked his body to break away from his cousin and explore: the details would have to wait.

Rob entered the old parlour, and instantly looked to his left and the view through the sash windows, while Mark moved to another room further down the hall. To Rob's right was a beautiful fireplace. The marble mantle was elaborately carved with a floral pattern; a ceramic vase sat on top of it, forgotten or unwanted.

'I've got something for you to look at,' declared Mark as he entered the room.

Rob turned to see his cousin carrying a framed picture. Mark attempted to blow some dust off it before handing it over. 'Meet your great grandfather, Thomas Mayfield.'

Rob gently took the framed painting. His eyes widened as he looked at an elderly man with a substantial grey beard.

'Thomas built this house,' said Mark.

Rob held the picture further out in front of him and then walked towards the window that looked down the valley. 'You picked a good spot Tom,' he said quietly.

The moment was broken by the sound of footsteps. 'Dad!'

'In here Jack,' replied Mark.

Jack entered the room red-faced: he was out of breath.

'Jack, where's Tom?'

Jack bent at the hips and placed his hands on his knees. He pointed towards the front door. 'I raced him.'

Mark glanced at Rob and raised his eyebrows.

'We saw you walk up here…so I raced him.'

Rob looked out the window to see Tom walking with the lethargy of a child heading towards the principal's office; his arms swung across his torso like elephant trunks, to further display his displeasure. 'I can see the silver medallist now,' said Rob.

'Can I show Rob the well dad?'

'No, I filled it in. Come this way Rob, I'll show you the old kitchen.'

Rob nodded as he smiled at the father and son exchange.

Tom Mayfield announced his arrival with heavy footsteps. 'Jack cheated,' he said, before sitting down to take off his boot. He tipped it upside down, and several small stones fell out.

Rob stared at the young lad. He realised that something had awoken inside him. He wondered if he could enact the change his life needed.

**

'Of course, it's possible Rob, but there is a lot to be talked through…agreed to,' said Gabi. The Sydney based lawyer stood up to leave her brother sitting in the two-seater cane lounge. She kept her back to Rob and wrapped one arm around a post that supported the awning of Mark's guest cottage. She looked over the green lawn and neat flower beds towards paddocks of sun-bleached grass. Too many scenarios ran through her mind to paint a clear enough picture about what her brother had asked.

'Well do you think they would at least let me work on the property…pay rent?'

It didn't happen often, but Gabi's heart broke for her stubborn, and sometimes obnoxious brother. He had been given a glimpse of a different life; for Rob, the prospect of heading back to his life in a northern England pub was akin to being sent to prison.

'Look Rob, all these things can be addressed. The first thing you need to do is go home and talk to Jan.'

Rob gave his sister a look that suggested something she didn't want to think about right now. She had just buried her father.

Gabi turned towards Rob. 'I will talk to Jim…just take the time to think through and everything will work out.'

Rob shook his head without making eye contact with his sister, and then stood up to move inside the cottage.

'Remember,' said Gabi, after Rob had opened the screen door to the cottage, 'Mark is taking us horse riding after lunch…it will be good to do something together.' She bowed her head, and then pinched the bridge of her nose, frustrated with putting her feelings aside to deal with her brothers. She thought of Natalie and decided she would give her a call.

**

Bradley lay on the sofa in the guest house and held a cold can of beer to his forehead. In his other hand he held a black glass button. He stared at it. He rolled it between his thumb and forefinger and then gingerly sat a little more upright. He had decided that the beer was no good as a cold press and took a mouthful. The ache, from his back to his toes, told him he would have trouble walking in the morning.

'What's that?' asked Rob, as he fell into the single-seater. 'Fuck, fuck,' he reached desperately for his foot. 'Cramp!' He sighed with relief when the contraction released. If that little Jack ever comes to England, I will make him haul kegs out of the cellar all day; he made those horses trot, I'm sure of it.' Rob felt a pain as he subconsciously acknowledged he would head back to his life in Hunslet. The jab to his pride had a bite worse than the cramp he had just suffered.

'He is a cheeky little thing isn't he, but very likeable,' said Bradley. 'It's a button.' Brad held his arm above his head so his brother could take it from him.

'Sorry, in a second. I'm not game to move,' said Rob.

'I found it in the dirt next to the creek when we watered the horses... I wonder how old it is?'

Bradley stared at the button again, and noted the intricate engraving that had been filled with dirt; he wet his finger with his tongue, and then polished. He decided that the button had belonged to a dress or some other item of women's clothing. His mind drifted to the book shop on Bene't Street. He wondered if Mr Andrews had repaired his Mum's book—Rob's book.

'I am going back to the creek in the morning with Mark,' said Rob. He looked towards the ceiling with his arms drooped over the side of the single-seater. 'Is it a creek or stream...it's too narrow to be called a river?' He rested his legs on the coffee table in front, and prayed that the cramps would stay away. 'Do you wanna come?'

Bradley craned his neck to look at his brother, and then looked intently at the glass button. It was the book and their fight that he actually saw.

'Mark is very confident he knows a spot where we will get a trout,' added Rob.

Brad acknowledged his brother's olive branch and decided to do something. He raised himself into a sitting position, and grimaced as he did.

'You too hey?'

'My backside feels like the horse kicked it,' said Brad.

Rob chuckled, and then yelped as another cramp hit. It wasn't as bad as the last. 'For Christ sake, what we were thinking…horse ride, yeh sounds great…little prick of a kid.'

Bradley laughed. 'He's not that bad. I think I will come to the creek…but I might just stand in it for therapy, they say it's pretty cold even at this time of year.'

'Maybe a good idea,' replied Rob, as he gingerly picked up a magazine from the lamp stand next to his seat. 'You might as well hold a rod at the same time.'

There was a moments silence while Brad gathered his thoughts. He was glad that he had spent some time with his brother and sister. The trip to Australia had been worth it for this moment alone. He suddenly remembered his father's funeral, the reason they were here; he felt bad, and then just as quickly, he didn't.

'Rob?'

'Yep.' The magazine couldn't engage him, so he flicked the pages with a child-like annoyance

Bradley took a deep breath. 'I got the book repaired, and I will send it to you when its finished…the whole thing was my fault.'

'Don't worry about it.' Rob flicked the next page a little harder. He was hit with images of their fight. It hurt him just as much, but he was better at putting it to one side than his younger brother.

Bradley searched for the right words. He didn't want to start an argument. He decided that there weren't any right words, just the truth. He had only acknowledged it himself in the last day or so. 'I just miss her.'

Rob didn't move, but the stillness betrayed his indifference. He missed her too, more than he would ever say.

'Sometimes,' continued Bradley, 'I question if my memories of her are real or...' He drank for longer than normal from his can. A few drops of beer dribbled from the corner of his mouth. He placed the button on the coffee table and then used his hand to wipe his mouth. 'I guess, I was jealous...I wished that she had left me that book.' Bradley pushed the button across the table with his index finger. 'Or, any book with my name written in it from mum.'

Rob sat still like the accused in an interrogation room. He stared straight ahead, not wanting to give a clue to what he felt. Whispers inside his head asked him to reveal it all, and free himself from the confinement of stubborn pride. The only page he had ever read in that book of poetry was the one in which his mother had inscribed his name. He knew everything about that page and he could see it as he stared blankly at the far wall. He knew, but didn't care that the book contained 1150 poems by 300 authors. It had been made at Oxford, a place, like Cambridge, so different to him, that he wondered why his mother had ever handed him the gift on that cold December morning. He still remembered, and could feel, the kiss she had given to his cheek.

After staring at the page, he had sometimes wondered about a quote on it: *poets by death are conquered, but the wit of poets triumphs over it.* He had even named his dog after the person who had written it, without ever really being bothered with who the person was. He had shown through his fight with Bradley that he cared deeply for the gift. The book was like a relic, something to draw strength from when all else felt weakened. Countless times he had lightly traced his hand over the words written by his mother, summoning memories and anything else that he could relate to the woman taken from them so cruelly.

Bradley waited for Rob to speak, and then used the armrest as support as he stood up. He picked up the button and then took a step.

'I am sorry for what I did Rob…I had no right.'

Rob went to reply, but it was no use. All the suppressions that allowed life to be bearable had developed defences that had protected and then soured him. He realised that the brother he teased and berated for his mildness was far tougher than he would ever be.

14

Cambridge

Karen cut the tape with her retractable safety blade and then ripped at the cardboard flap to open the box. Her enthusiasm for packing shelves had waned in the last ten minutes, and as a result she needed a second attempt to get the box completely opened.

As she stacked bottles of soft drink on the supermarket shelves, she began to think of her conversation with Brad and her spirits lifted. *Two more weeks, and this will be over, no more packing shelves,* she said to herself. The negativity that had taken hold of her over the years had a jab at her. *It will be the longest two weeks of your life.*

Her second phone conversation with Brad had been calm and relaxed, with no trace of the awkwardness that had been present the night before, or outside Heathrow Airport when they said goodbye. After Karen had assured her husband that everything was okay with Melissa, he had told her about the funeral at Adelong and the visit to the properties owned by his extended family: a small part being theirs. Neither of them had mentioned a move when he had first told her of what his father had left them, and were unlikely to after Bradley explained the intense heat that he had endured on his short stay.

They both continued to speak without the usual hurdles that interrupted their exchanges at home. Maybe it was the realisation that they didn't need to watch each penny now, or a sense of freedom from being parted. Karen hadn't dwelled on it, but the change was noticeable.

Melissa had sat on the sofa and wondered if it was in fact her dad on the line, by the way her mum spoke, and occasionally laughed.

Karen was aware of her animated responses, and she had noted a slight difference in Brad's voice too. He had sounded happy and there was a lightness to the way in which he responded to her questions. He still added a disclaimer to certain parts that highlighted how conservative he had become, like when he spoke of the cash left by his father. But Karen saw that as normal, he couldn't be expected to rejoice in his inheritance, regardless of how excited they both were to receive the windfall.

'$650,000, what did that come to in Pounds again?' she had forgotten. Karen lifted another carton off the trolley. She replayed bits of the phone conversation in her mind. They came to her out of sequence, and she wondered what the news would mean for them. It didn't mean retirement; she had already told herself that. It was a lot of money, but not that much, and she knew that she didn't want that anyway. She wanted to feel invigorated, like when she spoke to Alex, or when she had first travelled from Birmingham to Cambridge to study—she wanted to feel alive.

Brad's job wouldn't change, she thought to herself. Karen tried to remember if he had said that or she had willed it. *Anyway, it is too secure, and we will still need a steady income.*

Brad's voice had sparkled when he had told her about Rob and the wasabi oysters; it would become timid again, after a week of stamping forms at Cambridge Council, but the money would counter that, allowing them to do things that they haven't for the past, *how many years?* She regretted allowing that thought to enter her mind. *This is all positive.*

Karen looked at her watch. *Twenty minutes. A toilet break will use up five, maybe six.'* She pushed the trolley until she reached the soda water, and then walked to the rest room. She passed one of her work colleagues, who had thought of the same thing.

The conversation with Brad entered her thoughts again, and she smiled in a way that had been absent from her marriage for a long while. For more time than she cared to remember their lives had been dominated by fear. A state-of-mind that checked every consideration with the acceptance that any reward would be outweighed by the likelihood of failure. After all the talk about the money that had landed in their lap, the most endearing thing, the words that made Karen's heart feel warm, had come in one simple sentence.

'I want you to do something that makes you happy, Karen.'

Before he got off the phone, he told Karen that he would be two days later than planned. He also asked if they could tell Melissa together.

**

Cambridge

Karen stirred her coffee slowly without looking at it. Her eyes were fixed on the old chess player who was seated at his usual table closer to the door; his friend was late again, only the little man was not agitated today, he appeared lost, disconnected from the chessboard that lay in front of him. She looked at him closely and then realised that she never had before. He was plump around the cheeks, but his neck sagged, and like all old men, his ears were large. His nose was wide and thick around the nostrils. He had a mole on his right cheek, and Karen acknowledged that if he had shuffled down the aisle at the supermarket and asked what aisle the baked beans were in, she may not have recognised him.

The door to the coffee shop opened and Karen looked up to see Alex enter. They had arranged a morning catch up after Karen's shift because Alex had papers to write. Karen smiled at Alex, and Alex smiled back. She glanced at the old chess player, and her smile vanished. Alex stood for a moment and then walked towards the man, who had not even noticed the door open, and Karen knew at once what had happened.

Karen watched as Alex took the man's hand. She gently clasped it with her palm facing upward; the way someone might help another from the last step of a ladder. She leant over and kissed his cheek and Karen felt a lump form in her throat; she wiped a tear with her index finger, and then reached for a napkin to use in place of a tissue.

The man covered Alex's hand with his own, but continued to stare towards the traffic on Mill Road. Karen was overwhelmed by the kindness in Alex's act: the compassion, maturity, and awareness, to reach out to someone in need.

As Alex pulled up a chair to sit next to the elderly chess player, many thoughts raced through Karen's mind. Who was the man that she didn't know but had seen many times? She had grown fond of his mock agitation towards his friend, and their concentrations and animations over each move over the black and white chequered board. Those scenes had become part of her escape that was the coffee shop, but like a street play, she felt like the men were packed away, their lives frozen in time until she re-entered her little getaway. Was that all that they did, or had they led amazing lives; Karen being fortunate to witness the gentle and contented moments of retirement after a life well-lived.

She had never thought about the two men outside of what she saw in the coffee shop, but then why would she; she never gave one second of curiosity to the countless people who she assisted at work. Suddenly, and with a feeling that made her stomach tighten, Karen could see herself in that chair, alone and being consoled by someone she barely knew. Lately, she had imagined life without Bradley. In her mind it had all seemed uncomplicated, but the prospect of loneliness could cast enough doubt to accept the mundane.

Karen lifted her chin slightly and took a sharp inward breath to arrest her emotion, just as Alex stood and walked towards her. She felt giddy and anxious. She knew that she couldn't continue the way things were and be happy; apart from the small moments, she knew she already wasn't. She reminded herself that she had a husband, and a daughter who she had reconnected with. It didn't work.

Alex saw the look on Karen's face and took it as sadness towards the passing of Viktor. Alex had only learnt his name from Ben the barista the day before. She was glad that Ben had told her so she could offer Joseph her condolences. The old man had seemed surprised that Alex had known his name, but she hadn't let on that Ben had told her that too.

'Hi,' said Alex.

'Hi,' Karen's reply came out forced. It had had to negotiate the jumble of negative thoughts Karen pondered about her inadequate life. Bradley's news had given her a moment of exhilaration, but it was just that—a moment.

'Sad isn't it,' whispered Alex, 'to lose a friend after knowing them all your life.'

'Very.' Karen was embarrassed by her response. It lacked feeling, just like her marriage. It occurred to her that she had lost a friend as well, but it wasn't as sudden as it was for Joseph.

She glanced towards the man, conscious that he may have heard them talking. If he did, he hadn't let on. 'That was a very nice thing that you did for that man...he looks lost.'

Alex nodded politely and then looked towards Ben. He started to make her usual coffee. 'So, you said in your text you had some news?

Karen stared blankly for a moment. *I haven't decided yet,'* she said to herself. 'Oh, yes,' Karen's eyes became more animated. She felt a tingle run through her body. The sensation wasn't lost on her, and she wondered why she had reacted so plainly, so complacent, at home. She went to comfort herself silently with a word or two...but stopped. She had a sip of her coffee instead.

'Remember how I said my husband had to go to Australia for his father's funeral?' asked Karen.

'Yes, that is so sad,' replied Alex. 'How is he doing?'

'Good...I mean, under the circumstances.' Karen took another sip of coffee and reminded herself that it wasn't polite to act excited about receiving an inheritance, so she decided to reveal the part that she thought would interest her young friend. 'We own a farm in Australia.'

152

'Wow!'

'Well part own, with his sister and brother,' added Karen.

'Your usual Alex,' declared Ben, as he approached the table.

Alex lent slightly backwards, the sign language of coffee drinkers and diners that it was okay to complete the transaction. For a moment Ben imagined Alex looking at him with her almond eyes like there was no one else in the room. She would ask him what time he finished, and if he would like to go for a drink, and maybe dinner.

'Thank you, Ben,' Alex handed him a ten-pound note. 'Would you mind making a coffee for Joseph? Don't tell him it's from me.'

Ben smiled at Alex, not willing to trust his own reply.

Alex returned her attention to Karen. She placed her hand on Karen's hand, her eyes were wide and lit with interest. Karen froze at the warmth of Alex's touch; she almost allowed her thumb to lift and brush her friends palm. The thought horrified her, and the sensation left.

'A farmer, I didn't know your husband's family had a farm...how would I?'

Karen loved how Alex breezed through a gaff that would make her react self-consciously. The young university student made it seem like nothing at all, which is what it actually was.

'Well, I didn't either…well, not his father, I knew his mother had come from somewhere in the Australian bush, as they call it.'

'The outback,' said Alex in a strange imitation of an Australian accent. They both laughed. 'So, what does that mean for you Karen…are you moving there?'

'Oh, God no!' exclaimed Karen. I mean, we are not farmers.' She took a sip of her coffee to allow her abrupt dismissal to drift into some other corner of the room. She glanced to her left after she had seen Ben pass their table. He placed an espresso on Joseph's table and then sat across from him. He began to arrange the chess pieces. Karen thought the two young people in the room were deliberately trying to make her feel selfish.

'I am not exactly sure what it all means,' continued Karen. She looked back at Alex and noted Alex steel a glance at Ben. 'It is never a nice way to receive something, but I would be lying if I said it was unwelcomed…it will relieve the pressure a bit.'

Alex re-joined Karen, but she had been occupied with her own thoughts and had only half heard what Karen had said. Karen wasn't offended. She didn't expect Alex to understand the weight of domesticated life.

'Have you been to Australia Alex?'

'No, but I would love to…the Great Barrier Reef, Uluru; it all looks so cool.'

Karen thought about her last trip to Australia, ten years ago. It was good, but the plane trip alone had been enough to turn her off. The heat and the flies had made her mind up for sure. Maybe it wasn't all like that. The Great Barrier Reef definitely looked different to Adelong. She went to speak, and then stopped herself; she wanted to be more positive in front of Alex.

'It does, very colourful,' said Karen. 'Bradley said he would tell me more when he arrived home.' Karen had rehearsed what she would say to Bradley, over and over in her mind.

A moment of silence descended upon the two friends. Alex stared at her coffee: thoughts of her conversation with her grandfather suddenly entered her mind. Karen watched the young university student trace the rim of the cup with her finger, she could feel herself blushing, so she forced herself to look out the shop front window. To her relief, and distraction, a mother and small child were engaged in an argument the mother couldn't possibly win: she felt like she had seen the woman before.

'Karen.'

She heard Alex's voice, but took a moment to react. When she did focus on her friend her face gave that bewildered expression of a daydreamer. 'Yes.'

Alex reconsidered the question she was about to ask. She took another sip of her coffee and decided to proceed; certain things had scratched at conscience, things she hadn't considered before. 'Could I ask you something Karen?'

Karen did a jumbled calculation of what something could mean, but felt that she was in no position, for the sake of her friendship with Alex, to refuse the request. 'Yes, I suppose…what's on your mind?'

Alex looked towards the ceiling. Her chin lifted slightly to reveal another perspective in which Karen could admire how beautiful she was. Karen was flushed with feelings of envy towards Alex's youth, splintered by shards of embarrassment that she took such notice.

'What is it like to be married?'

Karen's preoccupation with Alex's features were washed away by a smell that didn't belong in the coffee shop. It was the scent of pans holding congealed fat and damp towels left on the bathroom floor. The smells were distinct from each other, but somehow lingered in the back of her throat as one: reminding her of the life she was yet to escape.

She sat stunned for a moment, not by Alex's question, but by how real and haunting the reminder was. Alex regretted asking.

'Sorry, that is too personal…I just thought you would be a good person to ask…I mean…'

Karen noticed Alex become flustered. It allowed her to forget about bland dinners and dirty laundry, and focus on her friend. 'Are you alright Alex?'

'Yes, yes.' Alex forced a smile. 'It's nothing really…I just had this chat with granddad.' Alex sipped her coffee. None of what she had said had played out like she had rehearsed; strangely it made her feel more adult, after the initial feeling of awkwardness.

'It is funny, you know,' continued Alex, 'I have spent so much time with him, and we get along so well…but suddenly I have all these questions. It sounds childish, but I feel like I don't actually know my grandpa.' She allowed the statement to hover for a moment. She realised how true her thoughts were. 'I mean really know him…does that make sense?'

Karen didn't answer straight away. She took a moment to consider how she could help her friend without revealing things about herself and her own marriage that could jeopardise the bond that they had made over coffee.

'I think I understand,' replied Karen. 'Obviously, I don't know your granddad, but you are very young…and I guess he would be seventy or eighty…it is natural that there are things about him that you wouldn't know. I suppose what's important, is how the two of you get on, and what you have done together.'

Karen felt a chill run through her body. She remembered the numerous times she had allowed her husband's hand slide off her shoulder. She would always turn just enough to make it happen, without the appearance of aggressiveness, but with the distinct absence of love.

'Your right, it's stupid of me…childlike really, to think my grandpa is perfect, but sometimes you have this idea in your mind of how things are, and then you suddenly have this gut feeling that it's not.' Alex felt she had said too much. By repainting the image of her grandfather, she could inadvertently smudge her own canvas, merely a sketch at this stage; something she hadn't considered, as she withdrew to her coffee. 'It's nothing, sorry to bother you Karen.'

'Not a bother at all.' Karen watched as the colour washed from her young friend's face. *It happens to everyone…disappointment. Just in different degrees,* she thought to herself. Karen stared at Alex unable to decide if she was saddened or relieved by what she had witnessed.

15

Sydney, Australia

The taxi stopped in the middle of the road for lack of parking spaces. The young driver hit a button on the meter with intent and then looked over his shoulder at Bradley and Rob. 'Twenty-five is close enough, he said.' The driver looked towards the row of apartments standing tall above rendered brick walls, and then quickly back at the two men in his vehicle.

Bradley glanced at the meter, as Rob got out of the cab, and thought of the friendly Greek after their lunch on the harbour foreshore. '$24.70,' he said silently. He placed a wine bottle on his lap and then handed over twenty-five dollars.

'What number is it?' asked Rob

'Twelve,' replied Bradley as he walked towards the intercom. He pushed the button and then waited. Static was followed by a muffled word. 'It's us,' said Bradley.

'Push the gate.' The was a metallic click that prompted Bradley to follow his sister's instructions.

**

Gabi greeted her brothers at the front door, and invited them into her apartment. Rob looked from behind Bradley and over his shoulder. He could see the harbour through large glass doors; the sparkling water surrounded by tree-

159

capped sandstone cliffs drew him past his siblings without the usual pleasantries given to someone on entering their home.

'Good afternoon Rob,' said Gabi, as he brushed passed her. She leant forward to kiss Brad on the cheek. He passed her the bottle he had purchased. 'oh, thank you Brad.'

'I wasn't sure, but I thought white would be good in this heat.'

Gabi studied the label. 'Perfect, come through and join your brother.'

Brad glanced around his sister's apartment and noted how ordered it was. The living room was lightly decorated, but everything that was there suggested Gabi was successful. 'The view is fantastic Gab.'

'Thank you, Brad.'

Rob nodded his agreement. He had accepted the luncheon invitation under sufferance: Gabi had insisted. *I have something I need to tell you before you leave*, she had said. Rob's mind had been preoccupied with his return flight to England the next day, and all that would come of it.

'Seeing as you are heading home,' continued Gabi, 'I thought we would have another seafood lunch…I went to the fish markets at Pyrmont this morning.'

'You're spoiling us, Gab,' said Bradley, as his older brother walked to the kitchen. He opened the fridge and helped himself to a bottle of beer. He tipped it towards Gabi as a substitute for asking.'

'I might open that bottle you brought,' suggested Gabi.

The sound of a door closing caught Bradley's attention. He turned to look down the hallway. 'That would be nice Gab,' he replied, his eyes were fixed on the woman walking towards them. She smiled, and then waved at Brad.

'Hello, I'm Bradley.' He took a step towards the woman and smiled. He offered his hand and she greeted him with confidence.

'Ah, you're ready!' exclaimed Gabi. She had overcompensated out of nervousness. She felt childish.

'I have heard a lot about you, Bradley,' replied Natalie. She glanced towards Rob, who took a swig of his beer. '…and you too Rob.'

Bradley turned towards his sister, nodded, and gave the softest of smiles. Gabi received her brother's message and felt relief wash through her body.

Rob nodded to acknowledge his name, and then took a step forward, as Natalie stepped gracefully across the lounge room to meet him. She smiled warmly, and Rob was won over, despite his efforts to remain aloof.

'Nice to meet you,' she shook Rob's hand softly, 'I was sad to hear about your father…' Natalie took a step back from Rob, and turned to look at Brad. Normally, she would walk up to Gabi and give her a kiss, she had teased that she would do something to shock her partner's brothers when they met, but she had realised the significance of this moment for Gabi, even though she saw it as slightly odd. She had seen the vulnerability in her lover, and her understanding of the constraints that had never inhibited her own life, had brought them closer together.

'...*I am sorry I never got the chance to meet him.*' Natalie was pleased that she didn't actually say what would have only hurt Gabi.

Gabi allowed her head to drop slightly, as if she had heard, and then regathered herself to focus on her guests.

She walked towards Bradley and took him by the arm, linking her free hand with Natalie. She kissed her on the cheek, and a thousand images rushed through her mind. She stared at Rob with purpose, and he moved his lips awkwardly. Gabi accepted that it was the best he could do for the moment. 'Why don't we have a drink on the balcony and enjoy the sun...I have some oysters to start with followed by scallops in a garlic butter, snapper...'

'...Sounds delicious,' said Brad, 'did you bring the wasabi for Rob?'

Natalie let out a laugh that took over the room, implicating Gabi, but breaking what little tension that remained in the room. Infected by her confident and alluring manner, Bradley and Gabi joined in, and Rob was outnumbered.

'Piss-off,' he said, more embarrassed than angry. He opened the sliding door to the balcony, and breathed in the salty air. Silently he thought about how different each of their lives were, and how much he wanted to change his. He said: *I am glad you are happy Gab*, knowing the words would never pass his lips.

'

16

The smell of old books greeted Bradley as he opened the door to Mr Andrews' bookstore. He felt at home. Two nights in the French city of Lille had refreshed him to an extent, but he still felt jaded after the long flight from Sydney. Bradley had diverted his homeward trip, motivated by his time with James.

After landing at Heathrow, Bradley had caught the train to Kings Cross and then hurried across the road to St Pancras Station, and the train beneath the channel to France. He had walked the battlefield of Fromelles and traced the steps of his grandfather and great uncle.

Bradley had stood in peaceful surrounds on an unfenced paddock and moved slowly in a circle; he took in the flatness of the ground, and tried to imagine what had taken place on that July night in 1916. *Somewhere on this field,* he had thought to himself, overwhelmed by what had been asked of the soldiers, *my great uncle died in battle. So far from home.*

The experience had humbled him. He remembered bending down to pick up some of the clay-like soil in a ploughed paddock that so many years ago had absorbed the blood and painful cries of thousands of Australian and British men. Bradley had crumbled the lump of earth in his palm, and somehow felt connected with a place he had never been to before; connected with his ancestors, and therefore himself.

The train from Lille back to St Pancras, and the continuation to Cambridge had been a good way to soak the emotional two days in. Bradley was looking forward to seeing Karen and Mel. He had so much to say, but he needed to go to the bookshop before he did anything else.

'Ah hah,' cried Mr Andrews, 'I thought you had left town Bradley.'

Bradley raised his briefcase slightly to acknowledge the book store owner before he placed it on the floor next to the hatstand. He removed his coat and then approached the elderly man who sat at the table which seemed to be his station for the classification of titles.

'Your book is finished my good-man, has been for a few days.'

'Thank you…sorry I haven't been in to collect it, but I had to go to Australia unexpectedly.'

Mr Andrews sat a little straighter, but still with the hunched shoulders that showed his age. 'Oh?'

'My father passed away.' Bradley looked at the ground and then at the shelves that surrounded him.

Mr Andrews choked back emotion. He was surprised at this own reaction. He had not really known Robert Johnson. He had met him once or twice, a polite handshake and a pleasant exchange, something he had done with many people; the difference being that he was the husband of the woman he had loved. 'I am very sorry Bradley.'

'Thank you, he had a good life.' A moment of silence descended over the shop while Bradley considered his statement. *What did I know of his life, apart from the fact that he was a doctor and my dad?*

'Yes indeed. Will you pass on my condolences to your brother and sister?'

'Of course, thank you…' Bradley's head tilted as though he had caught a strange sound in the distance. 'How did you know I had a brother and sister?' Bradley's question came out harsher than he had expected. He hadn't meant to challenge Mr Andrews; he had just been taken-a-back. The old man checked himself, a hundred memories flooded into his mind; he gave Bradley a vacant look.

'Sorry, Mr Andrews, I didn't mean to snap…I just couldn't remember if I had mentioned them.'

Gordon Andrews looked at Bradley while he summoned courage. His jaw sank, but not enough to part his lips; it made his cheeks appear to be hollower, it added age to his already wrinkled face. 'I knew your mother Bradley…in my university days, she was a wonderful and intelligent woman.'

Mr Andrews caught the lump in his throat with a manufactured cough, as Bradley tilted his head slightly. The elderly man's statement had caught him off guard and his peculiar reaction was a reflex way of absorption.

Bradley went to speak, but he stopped. He couldn't explain why he looked back towards the shop's front door and the large and warped glass panels that stood by its side, but he did. He stared for a moment and then looked back at Mr Andrews.

'I'm sorry…but you knew my mother, I…'

Gordon Andrews held up the repaired book as a way of explanation. 'This lovely old book Bradley…' Mr Andrews rested Bradleys prized possession on his lap and felt the passage of time through the texture of its cover…'I have seen it before. I apologise for not being more forthcoming, but it was a bit much to take in for an old man when I first made the connection…and then it just seemed….' Mr Andrews placed the book on the table in front of him and stood gingerly. He moved a coat, some loose papers, and then a stack of books to reveal a chair. He offered it to Bradley with a tilt of his head. 'It has been a long time.'

Bradley moved towards the table and then sat in the chair that Mr Andrews had provided. He was unsure of what he felt, so he sat for a moment without a word. He was both excited and confused by the news; he wondered why Mr Andrews hadn't simply said, *so, your Emma Johnson's son.*

'You know Mum passed away some time ago,' said Bradley softly as he twisted in his seat, 'cancer.'

Mr Andrews nodded solemnly as he pictured mourners at her graveside. He had stood back, at what he had felt was a respectable distance, and waited until Mr Johnson had led his children away before he placed a single rose at the headstone. 'I... the whole university was devastated when she passed.'

The elderly man ran the words through his mind that had always been written, or said in silence, except once, when he had uttered: *I love you,* and then wished he hadn't. Emma's mouth had widened and then closed while she had thought of the best way to reject without hurt.

Bradley looked from side to side at the columns of text and thought about his next question. He was young when she died, sixteen; not a child, but still too young to lose your mother. He remembered her, but was saddened that there wasn't more to call on. It was the same images that were played over and over.

As he sat and stared blankly, the piles of books seemed larger and he felt smaller; and like a boy, he fidgeted. He wanted to ask so much, but with each question that formed in his mind, the link between mother and son widened. It seemed to be an acknowledgement that he didn't know his mum in the way most people know the woman who nurtures and guides them. 'You recognised my mother's book?' said Bradley softly.

'It was the first time I met Emma...sorry Bradley, your mother. The book was the reason I said hello. Fancied myself as a poet at one stage.' Mr Andrews gave a warm smile. 'A flight of fantasy if ever there was one.'

Bradley laughed and relaxed. 'There is something about poetry that intrigues me.'

'Yes, that is a nice way to put it, Bradley. Did you study?'

'Yes, but not English, I should have studied history...I think. That is what I am interested in. I chose law instead.' Bradley screwed his face as he considered what he saw as his options at the time. 'Followed mum actually...it was either that or medicine.' Bradley's gut tightened at the memory of his father.

Mr Andrews looked at Bradley without comment, his mind floated between the man in front of him and his mother.

'But I ended up at a desk in local government.'

'Why did you quit?' Mr Andrews realised instantly that he had guided the conversation away from Emma.

Bradley's eyes widened at the direct statement. It was accurate, he had quit, but he was used to the book shop owner being softer in his approach to things. He paused before he answered. He wanted to be honest with Mr Andrews, with himself; he felt that he had developed a friendship, a bond. Bradley felt like he could talk with Mr Andrews in a way that he was never able with his own father; to suggest that he quit university because of an expected child, or financial security, would seem to do an injustice to their goodwill. 'It was hard…and I hated it.' Bradley felt a weight lift, not from his shoulders, as is often described, but from his chest. He felt like it had expanded. He realised that the notion of security and responsibility had been clung to, opportunistically, when he had needed an out.

Mr Andrews raised his eyebrows slightly. 'A good enough reason.'

Bradley glanced around the room as he considered what to say. 'My father didn't think so.' The Cambridge Council employee clenched his teeth. He wished he could draw in a breath and filter his last sentence back into his lungs; he had sounded like a teenage boy who had spoken without thought. Bradley decided to finish what he started. 'He thought I should have stuck at it.'

'May I ask why you started?'

'I…' Bradley let out a nervous chuckle, no one had ever asked him that question. Apart from knowing that he had somehow followed his mum, he had never really explored it himself. '…I just thought it was the logical thing to do…I thought it was what I was expected to do, with the grades I got that is.' Bradley smiled nervously at Mr Andrews. 'I always had good grades.'

'Would you care for a cup of tea Bradley?' Mr Andrews offered Bradley a life-boat.

'Yes, that would be nice.'

Gordon Andrews stood slowly.

'I will help.'

Bradley was politely refused with a raised palm. 'Relax young man, we have much to talk about,' he said, knowing that he couldn't talk about the mistakes he had carried with him for so many years.

The term young man, floated around inside Bradley's head as the elderly man shuffled away towards the rear of the shop. He stared towards the top of a mahogany shelf. He chuckled. *Young man, that's stretching the truth.* The irony was, that despite his own amusement, he felt like a young man in Mr Andrews' presence. He felt youthful and alert in his mind, tempted to explore new horizons, but also aware of his ignorance in what he had achieved so far.

Gordon Andrews sneaked a glance at Bradley Johnson as he shuffled towards him with a tray laden with a tea pot and cups. From the moment Bradley had re-entered his life, he had thought of the opportunity that had been presented. He had rehearsed how he might release his guilt and confess how his careless actions had hurt those around him, but he had suddenly realised how selfish his thoughts had been.

How could I do any good by transferring a burden of my own creation to another. Why would I hurt Bradley, tarnish the image of his mother, with a story about a foolish man and his ill-considered emotions. Gordon smiled at Bradley as he paused to steady to himself.

Bradley felt certain that something would topple from the tray that Mr Andrews carried. The fine china rattled like Cambridge had experienced an earth-tremor. He raised himself an inch out of his seat. *I could carry it the rest of the way.* He decided against it, smiled at Mr Andrews, and sank back into his chair.

Mr Andrews delivered the items intact, and eventually placed a cup in front of Bradley. He straightened and placed his hands on his hips before he inhaled and then exhaled, admitting to himself that it had been quite an effort. He smiled and then began to pour the tea. 'Milk?'

Bradley nodded.

'How long were you in Australia, Bradley? It seems like weeks since you were last in.'

Bradley sipped his tea, and then retracted suddenly from the hot liquid. 'Ten days or so…no twelve. I took a detour to France on the way home.' He wanted to ask questions about his mum, but the conversation had taken another direction. He restrained himself, feeling that it was the polite thing to do, the book shop, and Mr Andrews, had that effect on him.

Mr Andrews raised an eyebrow, and then blew gently on his tea before taking a sip. 'Fromelles via Lille,' said Bradley. 'My grandfather served there in World War 1. I learnt more about him while I was in Australia.'

'Ah…The Great War…as they would say. I was born not long after it all started.' Mr Andrews sipped his tea again. Although he had shifted the conversation, he pictured Emma Johnson next to him on a bench in the Scholar's Garden of St Johns, her face occupied the whole of his mind's-eye.

Sitting with Bradley in his bookshop, he could hear the rustle of leaves, as a strong autumn breeze pushed through the avenue of tall limes that guarded the sanctuary of the Scholars Garden. He could smell the air, and feel the roughened skin of a quince after Emma had looked left and right before she darted over the manicured lawn to pick it. He saw a man dressed without the gown of a fellow, appear and the disappear by the hedge at the garden's entrance. As he sat in his book shop, Gordon silently apologised for causing Emma's husband to doubt her.

Their friendship, and Gordon's love, would see them meet for robust discussions on literature, law, all matters of academia and on this occasion, family. When the weather permitted, the Scholar's Garden was a favourite place. Being close to Queens Road, Emma could ride her bicycle from Girton College, shooting along Huntingdon Road and Castle Street until she turned into Northampton. On more bleak days, a library, or on Gordon's suggestion, his office would suffice.

Emma Johnson had thrived amongst the learned surrounds of Cambridge. Inside Gordon's mind, her eyes sparkled as she waited for a response to a question long ago forgotten. In her lap, she held the book that Gordon would repair for her son many years later.

Bradley coughed gently.

Mr Andrews eased himself from his reminiscence. He looked Bradley straight in the eye, the way in which he wished he could have looked at his wife when she had found the letter to Emma. 'My father also served in that catastrophe. He was wounded; his knee shattered by shrapnel in his first action.'

Bradley grimaced. 'My goodness,' he said, not knowing what else to say.

Mr Andrews replied with a look that said he appreciated the effort.

'A blessing one would say,' added Mr Andrews, 'but in those days, and in a time of war, medical procedures were…well, he spent the rest of his working life with one and half legs.'

Bradley sat silently. His mind drifted back to Fromelles, the flat ground, the concrete German Bunkers; his imagination drawing black muzzled machine guns that tore into flesh regardless of their nationality or doctrine; the wasted humanity, and then the obvious question: why?

'I have often asked myself,' said Mr Andrews, 'was it his inability to work with the same capacity as other men that made him brooding and resentful in my childhood and adult life, or was it the fact that he came home and his three brothers didn't?' Mr Andrews paused for a moment, as if he was contemplating the question that he had already ceased trying to answer.

There was a longer silence, and Bradley saw the elderly man's eyes glisten as tears formed in them. Bradley looked into his tea cup. Thoughts of his own conflicts, and the desire for change in his life stirred from within.

Mr Andrews stood and made his way to his desk camouflaged with books, notes and receipts. He opened the small draw. He glanced at the unsent envelope, and then picked up the photo of Thomas, his son. Bradley watched him, as he shuffled back to his seat. He lifted himself from his chair without fully standing, as Mr Andrews offered the photo for him to look at.

Bradley studied the photo. He saw a man in uniform, proud, with a jaw set like someone who was intent on conquering whatever was thrown in front of him. 'Is this your son?' asked Bradley.

'Yes...yes, it is. The oldest of two boys...Thomas. Jonathon, Alex's father, he moved to Canada many years ago, he...' Mr Andrews stopped, and sipped his tea instead.

'It was a strange experience when Thomas said he was being deployed to the Falklands,' declared Mr Andrews. Bradley noted a change in his demeanour, he spoke with feeling, but in a measured way, like he was speaking to a larger audience. 'The news was abuzz about England defending its sovereignty, eight thousand miles away in the South Atlantic, but up until that point, I had never contemplated Thomas being involved.'

Mr Andrews used the armrest and his elbows to get more comfortable in his seat, he appeared to become more distant.

'I don't know what I was thinking really, when you consider he had been in his regiment for ten years, and had undertaken any course that had presented itself for advancement. The whole thing was just so far removed from who I was, and therefore who I thought my son was; the armed forces had just seemed like a job in an odd way, and then he was marching off, just as my father had.'

The bookstore owner withdrew in contemplation. He felt the irony of releasing one burden to Bradley over the other. He now realised that these things needed to be said too; probably a long time before this, but the fact that they were coming out in the presence of Emma's son, strangely didn't surprise him. In a way, he felt as comfortable in his presence, as he had with her.

He drew in a breath and held it momentarily before he spoke. 'People of my vintage,' he said suddenly, 'have seen so much conflict and devastation. It came to us in thirty-nine, even when we willed it to stay away...when we thought The Great War had put an end to the human race's fixation with killing each other.'

Mr Andrews sipped his tea. 'I will be the first to admit that I was a fool to applaud Prime Minister Chamberlain, when he embraced Heir Hitler's lies. In many ways, I am ashamed that I convinced myself to remain in Cambridge rather than take up arms...do my bit, as they called it...but I had seen what war had done to my father, and I didn't want it for myself. And I wasn't alone. Maybe' Mr Andrews corrected himself, 'we were afraid, but we knew that nothing good ever came from war.'

Bradley felt compelled to say something. He was a little confused by the direction the conversation had taken, but his unwillingness to seem apathetic, made his reply sound awkward. 'Was...Thomas killed overseas?'

Mr Andrews' attention suddenly focused back on Bradley. 'Oh, no...he survived...Thomas came back from the Falklands.' He contemplated Bradley's question further. He pictured Thomas on the dock-side, a shell of his former self. 'A part of him died on that island, most certainly, but he returned to us...for a while.'

The elderly book store owner looked around his shop from his chair, as if he had misplaced something. He stood slowly. 'I have taken too much of your time young Bradley, but I will be expecting a visit soon, we have much to discuss.'

Bradley felt lost for a moment. He felt a need to push the conversation further, or at least ask his elderly friend if he was okay. He stood and moved to shake Mr Andrews' hand instead. This talk had only hardened his resolve for change in his life. It now appeared so clearly to him that he had not lived, only survived. 'You must tell me more about mum's time at Cambridge,' said Bradley.

Mr Andrews smiled with his lips closed together. 'Don't forget your book?' The old man made for the table where the repaired and wrapped copy of *The Pageant of English Poetry,* rested. Bradley got there before him.

'Thank you, Mr Andrews.' A warmness ran the length of Bradley's arm as he picked up the old book; it filled his heart with the glow of reconciliation. *I will drive to Hunslet on the weekend.*

**

Alex entered the book shop from the back entrance. She checked a missed call from a friend and then dropped the mobile phone into a large hessian bag that she carried over her shoulder. It was a dull-brown except for some interesting artwork that she had drawn on it with coloured marker pens.

She spotted her grandfather seated behind his desk. His chin rested on his chest, and she immediately thought that he had fallen asleep. His thumb and forefinger moved to clasp each end of his eyebrows, and she stopped.

'Grandpa?'

Gordon Andrews didn't answer. He ran his hand through his whitish hair and then casually pulled out a folded handkerchief from his trouser pocket. He dabbed his eyes with it. Alex took a quick step forward, and then checked herself to move with more consideration—she had never seen her grandfather cry.

Alex came to his shoulder. 'Grandpa?'

He looked up at Alex and forced a smile; he felt too tired to conjure a plausible excuse for his display of emotion, so he covered Alex's hand with his.

'What's wrong grandpa?' Alex's eyes shifted downwards. She saw a letter in his lap, it had folds like a cross, and was tainted by age. An envelope lay on the cluttered desk next to a photo of a man in uniform: she recognised her uncle.

Gordon Andrews followed his granddaughter's eyes. *Would she understand?* he asked himself. He knew that it was unfair to expect her to, he never really understood himself;

he had just felt what he had felt, and then lived with the consequences.

His wife had never recovered from Thomas's death, nor had Gordon, what person expects to bury their child. Gordon had fought the bitter sorrow of loss with work at the university, while Celia had withdrawn into seclusion, emotionally paralysed by the pain of burying their son.

When Celia had knocked a book from Gordon's desk while cleaning one afternoon, a piece of paper had fallen loose. She had picked it up without breaking from her task, but had stiffened when the word Emma had leapt into her vision.

She had read, and then sat in disbelief as the words of her husband's love for another woman played over in her mind. She felt betrayed and humiliated; the foundations that she had built a life on had been shattered; her resolve, and then health, had collapsed.

Alex slowly picked the letter up. She noted the presumptuousness of her act, but continued anyway, too many questions had been raised lately not to. Her grandfather did not stop her, but he felt that he would never see Alex look at him in the way she always had since she was a little girl. After this, she would question his wisdom and doubt his advice. She would see what Celia had seen.

Gordon pinched the bridge of his nose, and then nodded to say: "*go on, read it.*"

She may move away, like Jonathon had, he thought to himself. *She might find it easier to receive the occasional phone call, than pretend at happy families.*

Alex read the letter and then allowed it to rest against her thigh, the paper contorted between her tense fingers. She had only known photos of her grandmother. There were many in her father's photo albums, but the one that had come to mind was of a young woman smiling like she had been told the most wonderful news. It sat framed on the bureau, in the dining room of her parents' Vancouver home. Alex suddenly realised that it was not accompanied by a similar image of her grandfather, and with a jab as distinct as a doctor's needle, she understood the distance between father and son.

Her grasp on the thin and unlined paper loosened, but not enough to allow it to fall to the ground. Her shoulders became more rounded as she felt the weight of being confided in; the side of life that people refer to as being adult, but is in fact just the act of being there or not; young or old, in good and tough times. She sat straighter.

'You loved this woman Granpa?'

He looked at Alex. Her eyes glistened but she was not crying. She reached for the envelope on the desk and placed the letter back in it; the man she had looked up to all her life, seemed frail and vulnerable.

He cleared his throat. 'I...never understood those words until it was too late, Alex.'

Gordon Andrews wrung his hands together, squeezing and then pinching at the regret. 'I wrote of love without regard for anyone but myself. I was a fool: a coward, and far from the gentleman I portray myself to be.'

Mr Andrews wiped his eyes again, but without the secrecy of before. 'I could say many things, but none of them matter, except for the fact that I broke my wife's heart.' The elderly man's body shook; the confession was released through a sob, and he looked towards the ceiling racked with guilt. 'I am sorry Celia,' he whispered. He clenched his fist and pushed it against his pursed lips.

Alex knelt beside her grandfather. Her mind told her that she should be angry at her grandfather. The words in the letter had left her in no doubt as to his feelings towards the woman. But instead, she felt pity. The pain on her grandfather's face was like nothing she had seen before, and her heart wept for him; she could not reconcile what she had learnt in the letter from what she knew of her past, but she could not help but feel pity.

'It's alright Grandpa,' whispered Alex. The words sounded bizarre to Alex, and they played over in her mind.

Gordon knew that it wasn't alright, but he appreciated Alex's compassion. He gently squeezed his granddaughter's hand. He felt shame for what he had done to Celia when she needed his support, and weak for burdening Alex with his regret. He had lived through words, and it was words, reckless and selfish, that had changed his life.

Deep inside, he felt the emptiness.

Alex stood and manoeuvred a chair as close as she could to her where her grandfather sat. Gordon Andrews removed a handkerchief from his trouser pocket, dabbed his eyes and then gently blew his nose.

'This lady, grandpa…she is that man's mother?'

Gordon nodded.

Alex began to speak, but she felt that what she was about to say was only window dressing. She cleared her throat. 'Does dad know?

Her grandfather nodded again.

Alex allowed her right foot to move like a pendulum, but much slower. Her brand-name sneaker lightly brushed the worn timber floor. She thought as deeply as her age and experience would allow. She tried to summon anger, but she hadn't had the relationship with her grandmother to fuel the emotion. All she could see was her distraught grandfather, and it was pity that came in waves: she felt a need to nurse, not judge.

'I don't know what to say grandpa, but I love you.' Alex stood, and in an action that took her by surprise, she bent at her waist and kissed the elderly man on the top of his head before allowing her cheek to rest on his. She was confused as to how she should be acting. She thought about her parents, and how she would react if it was her father. Her overwhelming sense was to be there for her grandpa, so she stood and walked towards the kitchen.

'I will make some tea,' she said.

17

Bradley placed his suitcase on the ground and then knocked on the front door of his home; it felt odd not to have his own keys to carry out the task that had become part of the routine. He heard footsteps, and the door opened.

'Dad!'

'Mel,' He leaned in to hug his daughter. The carry bag Gabi had given him to hold gifts in, swung from his shoulder and hit Melissa in the leg.

'Ouch!'

'Sorry luv.'

'What's in that,' she asked, exaggerating a limp while smiling. She was truly pleased to see her father.

'Presents!' Bradley picked up his suitcase and stepped through the doorway. He looked up and saw Karen. Bradley though she looked different…younger maybe. Karen noticed his reaction. 'Hello Kaz…you look nice.'

'Welcome home Brad.'

Bradley went to speak, but Mel jumped in.

'Mum had her hair done.'

'Yes Mel, I noticed. It looks great, Karen.'

'Do you like it? Asked Karen, she wanted confirmation.

'I do.' Brad was unsure how far he should take the compliment. If he said it made her look younger, would that mean he was saying she had looked older before. Was it one of those lose-lose situations? He threw caution to the wind; he was just pleased to have been greeted with warmth. 'You look younger, the darker colour suits you.'

Karen smiled warmly. 'Do you think so?' She hadn't been sure about Alex's advice, but she had been right.

The married mother of one, former university student and supermarket worker had made her mind up that her marriage was over, or had eroded away to the point where it was a working arrangement. Seeing Joseph in the coffee shop had shaken her. She had asked herself if she had just got complacent, and decided that she needed to try harder.

On the walk home from her getaway, Karen had passed a hairdresser that she had never used before. She looked at the glossy photos in the window, and then felt foolish when she rang Alex for a confidence boost. When she left the salon, she walked along the pathway looking people in the eye, instead of staring at the cobblestones. She felt good, and wondered why she had let herself slide. A little voice barked back at her: *The money helps.* She ignored it, and told herself that when Bradley came home, she would tell him about her plans. She wanted to do something with the life she had left.

'So, how was the flight…and France?' Karen tripped over the words. She had been shocked, and then pleased that her husband had made the unexpected deviation, it hadn't made her cranky—just surprised her. Her old attitudes, or the ones that had grown with time, had initially grabbed her, and asked questions; suspicious and self-centred questions, which had more to do with her own insecurities than Bradley.

'The flight was long, but going to Fromelles was very worthwhile. Tony, my cousin, knew so much, and I thought if I don't do it now, I never will.' Bradley noticed Melissa shifting her weight from one foot to the other.

'I am glad you did that,' replied Karen, 'you have always been interested in that sort of thing.' Karen winced at her choice of words.

'You have some gifts?' interjected Melissa.

'A couple,' said Bradley.

'I wanted to go to France as well, but I wasn't allowed, was I?'

Bradley noted the change on the home front. What had been said with screams, was now said in jest.

'Why don't we sit,' suggested Karen.

Bradley smiled, picked up the carry bag, and moved to the sofa to sit next to his wife. 'Before I get out the

187

presents, be warned they are not that great. Sydney is a beautiful city, but the gift stores are a bit tacky.'

'What about Adelong dad?' asked Melissa in a mock Australian accent.

'Be nice Mel, they are your cousins. Actually, they had a great gift shop…but before I start, there is something I would like to say.'

'I am not moving to Australia,' said Mel.

Bradley rolled his eyes. 'Relax Mel, we are not moving to Australia.'

Karen realised her jaw had clenched involuntarily at her daughter's statement. She also had something to say. *What did Brad want to say?* Her inner voice was alarmed.

'Seriously, I had a lot of time to think while I was overseas.'

'I was only joking dad; I was sad that your dad died.'

'Thank you, Mel, that means a lot.' Bradley picked up the carry bag and put it next to him on the sofa to recalibrate his thoughts. 'I thought about us as a family, and…look, I am hopeless at this,' he looked straight at Karen.

Her pulse began to race. She had rehearsed what she was going to say. *Your being selfish Karen.'*

'Kaz, if you would like to, I was thinking you could leave your job at the supermarket, and maybe do something you want to do…something different?' In a sub-conscious act, Bradley spread his hands and then clasped them together. 'What do you think?

Karen sat silently. She didn't want to cry, "*something you want to do*". Her face fell to focus on her lap and Bradley wondered if he had assumed too much. Thoughts raced through his head, his trip to Australia, the dullness that he had been accustomed to, the money, Karen's new, and almost black hair. She sniffled, 'I would like that very much.' With her elbow on her knee, and her head rested on her palm, she cried.

'Are you alright mum?' asked Melissa.

Bradley put his arm around her. He put his mouth close by her ear, and said 'I love you.'

She went to say the same, but gripped his forearm as a substitute.

'I will try harder Karen,' said Bradley.

Karen lifted her head. 'So, will I Brad, I really will…'

Brad kissed his wife, and then wiped her tears with his thumb.

'Oh my God, I am going to be sick,' said Melissa. She stood and walked to the kitchen in protest at her parents' show of affection. Silently she felt very happy.

Karen turned to Bradley. 'This might sound crazy, but I was thinking of finishing my English degree…or start all-over. I have found my passion for it again. I am not sure what I have to do…'

'We will work it out,' said Bradley. 'I think it's great. I have a few ideas, but I think we better look at these presents. Mel, what are you like with a Boomerang?'

In the warm surrounds, Mel felt comfortable enough to revert to being a teenager. 'I knew it,' she moaned.

Bradley and Karen laughed. 'Look it's the real thing.'

'You didn't get me one, did you,' asked Karen, putting the joke to one side.

'No, I didn't, but you have to promise to wear this.'

Mel shrieked with laughter after her dad produced a green and gold coloured woollen jumper, and suddenly felt better about her Boomerang. 'It's so bright; where are my sunglasses.'

**

Hunslet, England

Rob flicked the tea towel he carried over his shoulder and then picked up a stool, flipping it in one motion before placing it gently on the bar. He took one step towards the next one, and did the same: he continued until he reached the wall that held the notice board.

He moved closer to the multi-coloured pamphlets, and stared at one in particular. 'That was a month ago, 'he said, before ripping it from the pins that held it. He scrunched the paper into a ball, and then shoved it into his tracksuit pocket.

He noticed a pair of reading glasses on one of the tables, and let out a sinister chuckle. 'You stupid prick, Barry, I wonder how far you got before you...' Rob realised he was talking to himself. He quickly whipped the tea towel from his shoulder with his right hand, as he heard the back door to the bar open. 'Closed,' he said. He had mastered that single word over the years to make it sound as menacing as possible. 'Oh, it's you...I thought you'd gone to bed.'

'Couldn't sleep.'

Rob nodded, as his wife took a stool from the bar to sit on. 'He had said everything that he had wanted to say, before he had started his evening shift. The regulars knew him well enough not to ask questions when he was in a mood, and they had not asked any that night.

'Can we talk?' asked Jan.

Rob shrugged, flicked the tea-towel over his shoulder again, and then removed another stool from the bar. Jan looked odd dressed in a nightgown in the bar. He laughed.

'What?'

He pointed to her baby blue cloak. She looked down, and let out a soft giggle of her own. 'If only the locals could see me now.' There was an awkward silence that made Rob feel tense. He clenched his jaw to prevent himself from saying anything. He was not known to back down from an argument, but he didn't want another for the sake of it.

'I was thinking about what you said...before, and you are right,' she added quickly.

Rob was not sure what he had prepared himself for when his wife appeared in the bar, but it wasn't what he had just heard. He chose to remain silent.

'This place has us by the throat,' she continued, 'but it's all I know.' Jan brought her hands together to rest in her lap. She looked down: the thumb of one hand gently massaging the back of the other. 'I've never thought of leaving it...' she glanced at the beer-stained carpet, the dull patterns conjured a thousand images. 'Well, I have, but never seriously.'

'Jan...'

'Rob!' Jan interrupted her husband, she wanted to be the one to say it, she felt her husband deserved that. She realised it while they had argued, and admitted to herself while she had lain in bed that it had always been what she had wanted, or what her insecurities wouldn't entertain. 'I will go to Australia with you...I am scared, but I will go...the boys are adults now.

'Well Matt is,' said Rob in jest. He felt like his whole body had split as he smiled; he couldn't remember a feeling like it…ever. He put his hand over his brow like a man shading his face from light. He felt loved. He felt happy, and he hugged his wife. 'You'll love it Jan…and if you don't, we will come back. Thank you, Jan.'

The words were muffled against her night gown, but Jan heard them; she too, felt loved.

Part Two

18

Cambridge, two years later.

Karen put the washed plate, cup, knife and then fork back in their respective places. She looked out the kitchen window and watched two kids playing. The view beyond the children was pleasant. Jesus Green was always nice this time of year; she just wished the window was bigger, then she might be able to see the River Cam.

The rent was an issue, even for a one-bedroom place, but Bradley helped out. Karen began to pick at her nails. It had been more than a year since they had split up: three weeks since the divorce had been finalised. The excitement of financial freedom and a new beginning had brought happiness, and then the winds of change had lulled.

Karen had resumed her studies and Bradley had continued his work with the council, using his spare time to indulge in his passion of history. As a family they had picnics on the Cam, and trips to London, but the periods where it was an effort to find something to talk about became more noticeable, more like it had been, for the husband and wife.

During Karen's busy periods, Bradley and Melissa would entertain themselves while Karen pursued her new goals. Like a passenger staring at the dock from a boat's stern, she had watched them together, while she willingly drifted further away.

She jumped after she had dug too deep near the quick of her fingernail. The pain ceased her day dream for the moment, and she looked back out the window to see that the children had moved on. In the almost complete quiet, Karen lifted the electric kettle from its cradle and turned the tap on; she tried to estimate enough for one cup, but usually found herself filling it halfway.

The noise was one of the things she missed the most, or the prospect of it. After her fling with Martin had ended, it was the first thing she noticed. The quiet made her think, and when she thought, she was reminded of what she had lost.

Bradley's inheritance had seemed like a salvation at the time, but the feelings that she had carried for so many years until that moment, had become too entrenched to be filled-in by something that was superficial. The money had opened a door to new and exciting things, an opportunity to reclaim lost ground, and they had grasped at it, as if the lack of talking, loving and caring had ever formed to be a barrier in their marriage.

Karen met Martin at her first tutorial, he was ten years younger, but on the same path: making up for decisions made and regretted. Coffee was had, but unlike with Alex, it eventually moved to a drink in a bar, and then dinner. One night, they had sex on Martin's dining room table, and Karen felt the adrenaline of breaking conceived entrapment. In that period, within the walls of Martin's flat, they had much in common. They studied at a college that offered a bridge to further studies at Cambridge University; their common subject seemed to provide an endless line of conversation.

She was engaged in the excitement of discovering new frontiers; stimulated by his unencumbered masculinity, and the prospect of becoming the woman she always thought she would be. He was someone who was enjoying the moment, sincerely and in good faith, but without any notion that there was an idea of commitment.

Karen had not considered what it would mean to her home life; her time with Martin and the path to fulfilment had swept her away quickly, and it felt good, just as the erosion of her relationship with Bradley had felt bad: slow and painful.

A different pain to the one she felt when Melissa and Bradley had found her with Martin in their own home, after they had returned early from a trip to the coast. Melissa had remembered the moment with her boyfriend two years before, and her mother's reaction; she was stung by the hypocrisy, far worse than the sting of her mother's palm on her cheek.

At eighteen years of age, Melissa was more independent; hardened by her up and downs as a teenager, and what she saw as betrayal to their small family by her mother. Over time, Bradley had tried to absorb some of his daughter's anger towards Karen, telling his daughter that marriage was difficult, and he had played his part in what had happened, but none of the confessions about complacency and fear made any sense to the young adult. If anything, it just made him appear saintlier, which in turn had tightened her relationship with her dad.

Melissa had taken her trip to France, but not with Toby. Bradley had told Karen she had gone with a young man she had been seeing for about six-months, an apprentice carpenter, Tom. Karen had to rely on those bits of information from her ex-husband, so she could paint an image of Melissa in her mind; her daughter never returned her calls, and had crossed the road one day to avoid her mother when she was near the old Round Church.

Karen moved to her lounge room, which was almost part of her kitchen. She sat down and glanced at her text books, she turned the television on. She thought about walking to the Mitre on Bridge Street. They had nice meals, she could eat early and have a glass of wine; there was usually some sort of atmosphere there. She dismissed the idea, the thought of eating-out alone was more depressing than no one knowing you were eating alone at home.

Gilmore, near Adelong, Australia

Rob stood for a moment and watched his wife, as she looked down the valley. She sat quietly, almost frozen, while the morning sun slowly rose to spread its arc of warmth towards their new home. Two pillars of steam lifted from the mugs

Rob held; the view of cattle that grazed on green paddocks, against the smell of eucalypts and dewy grass, had made Rob feel more at home with each day that passed.

They were both dressed the same: jeans and flannel shirt, the only difference being the variation in the spots of paint on the old items of clothing. Rob scuffed his work boots on the verandah boards as he stepped towards Jan, and she was startled.

'Cup of tea before we start,' he said.

'Thanks Rob,' Jan's thick Yorkshire accent a reminder to Rob of their journey together, and the sacrifice that she had made for the sake of their marriage. 'I can't believe we're almost done.'

'One more room,' replied Rob, as he took a seat next to his wife on the cane lounge, a housewarming gift from his cousin Mark that his wife Bec had picked out. 'Like you said, it took a while, but we saved money doing it ourselves mostly.'

Jan didn't reply immediately; she was thinking of her sons. She was happy, but the distance between her and her children was something that was unnatural for a mother, and a problem that she would like to find an answer to. The mention of the money that they had saved in renovating Rob's grandparents' homestead had allowed a thought to resurface.

'It would be nice for the boys to see this place, Rob…after all the work we've done. It would be nice for us to see them.'

Rob understood, and had for a while. They had been busy working on the farm, renovating their home; both of them working part-time to prolong the inheritance that building supplies and tins of paint had dug into. They had made decisions together, and carved out a new life.

Rob often thought about the man who had almost resigned to the life that he had been dealt. In the evenings, he would watch rusted skies turn to star-filled nights and wonder if the vast expanse of this country had absorbed the anger, and hate, that he had often felt. He didn't consider himself born-again, the currents that drove his personality were still there, but it rolled like an open ocean instead of crashing like surf on jagged rocks.

As happy as the transition had been, Rob had recently seen his wife staring at old photos, and writing letters that were often not answered. He thought of his relationship with his own father, and the one he had with his two boys; the lack of effort, which had passed from one generation to the next.

His decision had been expensive, but he had made a call that he knew his wife wouldn't object to.

Rob had a sip of his tea, and decided that the surprise would be just as good now as he had planned it to be in two months' time. 'It will be,' he said, 'I'm looking forward to it.'

Jan smiled with her husband's words. She sipped her own tea, enjoyed its warmth, and then slowly turned to her husband. 'What do you mean you're looking forward to it…' Her face was a mixture of joy and anguish. She held at bay a wave of emotion that she feared had been built on wishful daydreams. 'What have you done Robert Johnson?'

'Oh nothing.' He smiled at his wife. He wanted to draw out the suspense, and feel the emotion he had often denied himself when his mind was dominated by anger.

Jan pushed him in the chest playfully with an open palm. 'You're being a shit, Rob.'

'Jan, you're not going to fly off the handle, and get angry, are you?'

'I'm already angry.'

Rob laughed as he watched the daughter of a Yorkshire publican bristle, it reminded him of their very early days, when tension was turned into something primal and exciting. 'Well…I should have asked you first…with the money, and all, but I bought Matthew and Billy plane tickets.' Rob casually took a sip from his mug. He smirked as the warm liquid slid down his throat. He kept one eye on his stunned wife. He finished his teasing with one last sentence. 'To come and see us for a bit.'

Jan put her palms together; she placed them over her mouth and her nose, and took in a sharp breath. A tear rolled down her cheek. 'Oh…' she tried to speak, but took another sharp breath instead. '…I have missed them, Rob.' She leaned into her husband and rested her head on his chest.

'So, have I,' he replied. The words had come out in order to comfort his wife, but as he looked down the valley, he realised that he truly had. Taking in the view before him, he reflected on how his life had played out. It was hard for him to remember how he had ever come to be confined within the walls of that pub. Was it the pub, or did he let it all happen: a willing victim to his own contempt for anything that was close to him?

He thought of his father, and how he had allowed him to pass without reconciling, or even relieving his conscious of what he felt; preferring instead to drift apart, as if there was never a connection in the first place.

He thought of his mum, and felt that she would be pleased with him, now at least; maybe not before, when he was self-centred, and angry. He still got angry, from time to time, but it was mostly superficial, not anger as in bitterness that comes from holding things inside, like the loss of his mum.

'C'mon,' said Rob, 'this room won't paint itself, and I have to work at the club tonight.'

Jan sat up and placed her hand on her husband's face. She smiled, 'Thank you, Rob.' She kissed him on the cheek.

They stood together and hugged, before they walked along the verandah and towards the French Doors that led into the bedroom they were about to paint.

**

19

Lille, France

Bradley walked past the entrance to a shopping mall. He could see the Gare de Lille up ahead, so he stopped to consult the map the hotel receptionist had given him. He turned the map around; looked up at the train station, but was distracted by two young girls standing in front of him. They held coffee cups, and Bradley immediately noticed the dirt in and around their finger nails that gripped the well-used containers.

One girl shook the cup, and took a step closer to Bradley, while the other gave a look of sorrow that the middle-age man found hard to ignore. He reached into his pocket and put one Euro into each cup. The girls were pleased and ran away. Bradley felt good, and then suddenly naïve. The girls, or one of their friends, would be back, now that they had found a tourist who was generous.

He glanced at the map again, and saw the road he was looking for: *Rue Faidherbe*. He reached into his trouser pocket and read the elegant handwriting of his friend, *Vieille Bourse*.

"We will meet at the old stock exchange and have some brunch," Mr Andrews had said. The bookshop owner had risen early, and his suggestion had reached Bradley, but been muffled by the pillow that covered his head. The note left on his bedside table that Bradley now held, had been

appreciated, but as the amateur historian saw the young girl with the coffee cup and an older boy circle behind him, he started to think he should have risen with his travelling companion.

Bradley found Lille to have an energy that was hard to discern. He felt intimidated by the crowd, and as he walked, he found himself looking anxiously from left to right, making him appear more like a tourist than the map and his donation already had.

As he walked past the Gare de Lille, he quickened his step to cross the busy street. A stream of cars sped toward him, but he felt compelled to continue as he caught sight of a group of youngsters who he had identified as potential beggars, but in truth may just have been locals waiting for a bus.

He felt his pulse race, and cringed with the indignity of being frightened by children, but the comfort as he reached the paved Rue Faidherbe was undeniable, and after twenty metres or so he had relaxed into a more confident stride. He appreciated the softer architecture of apartments atop of cafes and boutiques with steady, sweeping glances, instead of the bird-like proddings of before.

Bradley continued, and with each step, he felt less the tourist, until an attractive young French lady stopped him near the Opera de Lille and asked him a question. He had caught the words, Euro Lille. He regretted spoiling his charade by attempting to say, *"je ne parle pas francais."* He should have just appeared rude and pointed.

His cover blown; Bradley reached for his map again. He had not ventured this far on his last stay in the French city. He took his bearings from the opera house, and with a one-hundred and eighty degree turn he realised his destination. The Vieille Burse was a striking and beautiful building, as were all those around him, and although there were pedestrians everywhere, he felt more at ease, like he was in a different city to the one he had encountered around the train station.

Eager to meet with his friend, Bradley walked quickly towards the seventeenth century building and caught a glimpse of bright red umbrellas that told him he was in the right place.

The Rue de Manneliers; its quaint apartments with narrow wrought iron balconies, opened into a town square. The area was busy with people walking or sitting around the tall monument in its centre, and Bradley was captivated by a scene that had been replayed over hundreds of years, the only difference being the costumes of the actors.

Bradley took a moment to take in the energy of the thoroughfare, and then casually looked to his right. Mr Andrews sat with one leg crossed neatly over the other. He sipped his coffee, and then continued to look across the busy city square.

There was a dull flutter and then a grating noise as Bradley pulled back the chair from the table. He stopped. *I broke the rubber grommets.* He lifted the chair slightly, and Gordon smiled at him. The former professor of English had come to know Bradley quite well over the last couple of years; it was acts like the one he had just witnessed, that had warmed his heart when it had been chilled by loneliness and the reflection of what his life had become.

'You made it?' said Gordon. He took another sip of his coffee, glanced at a small package on the table addressed to Alex in Canada, and then back at Bradley.

Bradley raised his hands slightly to admit his tardiness. 'Sorry, I slept in. This is nice.' Bradley looked around the square again, and then jerked his head in the direction from where he had come. Gordon laughed.

A waitress appeared at Bradley's side.

'La carte, monsieur.'

'Thank…merci,' replied Bradley. He smiled sheepishly.'

'Cinq minute?'

Bradley realised he had been asked a question, and in his flustered state had even thought he had recognised a word, but he couldn't be certain. He smiled and nodded, and then Gordon intervened.

'Bonjour mademoiselle.'

'Bonjour monsieur.'

'Cinq minutes, seraient bien…merci.'

Bradley took a deep breath and held it. He looked at the waitress and smiled and then at his friend in an attempt to contribute to the exchange. He was surprised at how helpless he felt.

'You looked concerned, Bradley,' said Gordon, as the waitress walked away.

Bradley exhaled: he took a moment before replying. 'It sounds silly, but I felt so confident with my French lessons, but the simplest thing can be difficult.'

Gordon smiled and nodded. 'Glad to help.' He took a sip of his coffee. 'You have been here before, haven't you?'

'Yes…but no, really. I got off at the train station last time from the airport, walked across the road to the hotel, and got picked up in the morning by a guide who spoke perfect English. I was dropped off, and then caught the train to St Pancras…so I haven't really been here, been here.' Bradley pointed to the ground to make his point.

'I didn't order you a coffee, Bradley.'

'That's fine.' Bradley turned in his chair. He looked through a gap in the red umbrellas to look at the beautiful building that cast a shadow over them. The orange-brown paintwork was highlighted by the soft yellow that surrounded the rows of grey-framed windows that appeared as large as doors. 'The façade is magnificent Gordon.' Bradley had stopped calling him Mr Andrews after Gordon had suggested it politely one afternoon in his bookshop.

'La Vieille Bourse…the old stock exchange, and it is truly splendid,' replied Gordon. 'Seventeenth Century…Spanish, would you believe…until Louis XIV took it back.'

Bradley turned back to face Gordon. 'Spanish…here?'

'Yes, the whole region was controlled by the Spanish, hence the architecture. Not the chocolates though.' Gordon lightly tapped the box addressed to Alex. 'Very much Belgian.' Gordon pointed towards the monument in the middle of the square. 'There are some lovely cobble-stoned streets over there, I had a look while you were at the hotel…we can go back after we eat.'

Bradley turned slowly towards Gordon to acknowledge his suggestion, but his mind was somewhere else. His friend's revelations about the change that the city had undergone over centuries had made him think about the change that had been undertaken in his life.

At times he missed Karen, but he often questioned if it was just having someone there: someone or something to help hold together the structure of an existence. He certainly missed the woman he had fallen in love with, but that couple had drifted apart long before he had asked Karen for a divorce. He had even contemplated a reconciliation, and had almost suggested it; relieved that he hadn't when the image of her in bed with another man flashed before his eyes.

The evenings were quiet when Melissa wasn't at home, which was becoming more frequent, but he felt stronger in himself and he was emboldened by the freedom he felt from the lack of constraints, imagined or imposed, that allowed him to live as a single man.

Gordon looked up, and the waitress appeared as if on cue. He leaned closer to Bradley. 'I wouldn't mind driving across the border tomorrow to Ypres, if we have time…after Fromelles?' Have you been there?'

'That would be nice,' replied Bradley.

'Done.' Gordon turned his attention to the young waitress. 'Mademoiselle.'

She smiled politely at the tourists.

**

Other Titles by E. J. Williams

Weakest Moments